CRACKS
IN THE
CONE

CRACKS
IN THE
CONE

Coco Simon

Simon Spotlight
New York London Toronto Sydney New Delhi

This book is a work of fiction. Any references to historical events, real people, or real places are used fictitiously. Other names, characters, places, and events are products of the author's imagination, and any resemblance to actual events or places or persons, living or dead, is entirely coincidental.

SIMON SPOTLIGHT

An imprint of Simon & Schuster Children's Publishing Division
1230 Avenue of the Americas, New York, New York 10020
This Simon Spotlight edition May 2018
Copyright © 2018 by Simon & Schuster, Inc.
All rights reserved, including the right of reproduction in whole or in part in any form.
SIMON SPOTLIGHT and colophon are registered trademarks of Simon & Schuster, Inc.
Text by Tracey West
For information about special discounts for bulk purchases, please contact Simon & Schuster Special Sales at 1-866-506-1949 or business@simonandschuster.com.
Designed by Hannah Frece
The text of this book was set in Bembo Std.
Manufactured in the United States of America 0318 OFF
10 9 8 7 6 5 4 3 2 1
ISBN 978-1-5344-1750-2 (hc)
ISBN 978-1-5344-1749-6 (pbk)
ISBN 978-1-5344-1751-9 (eBook)
Library of Congress Catalog Card Number 2018934108

CHAPTER ONE
SPRINKLES SELFIE

My best friend Allie squeezed my hand. "Happy Sprinkle Sunday," she whispered to me. Then she whispered the same thing into our other best friend Sierra's ear. I could sense both the nervousness and the excitement in Allie's voice. *Sprinkle Sunday*, I repeated in my head. It was finally here. And I did mean finally. I felt like we'd been waiting *forever*—even though it had only been a week since the last time we had all been here.

Allie's mom, Mrs. Shear (or, as I called her, Mrs. S.), had opened an ice cream shop after she'd divorced Allie's dad, and Mrs. S., Allie, and Allie's little brother had moved to another town. It was a whole lot of change, especially for Allie. But we were all really happy when Mrs. S. offered the three of us (that's me, Sierra, and Allie) jobs at the ice cream store every Sunday. That was why we called ourselves the Sprinkle Sundays sisters.

Aside from our making some extra moolah (which my mom said should go toward a college fund, but I had other ideas) with the new gig, Mrs. S. had given us all cute T-shirts to wear with the shop name, Molly's Ice Cream. (Molly had been Allie's great-grandma, and she'd taught Mrs. S. how to make ice cream and had inspired the shop.) Plus, I got to spend some quality time with my two besties. I'd been super-excited about it all week. Until . . . well, until Sunday morning happened.

I was almost late for work, which would have been bad, because the previous week at our trial session Sierra had been super-late, and Mrs. S. had made it clear that it shouldn't happen again. But I slept through my alarm because I'd stayed up customizing my toilet seat with plastic fish and mermaid charms. It looked really cute, and it was going to make for a funny surprise for my guests. (Don't judge—it was Allie's idea, and it came out awesome.)

Anyway, I woke up to find Mom shaking me.

"Tamiko! You have to get ready," she said.

I groaned and pulled the pillow over my face. "I think there are laws against waking up children by shaking them. It's cruel and unusual," I said.

Mom made a grunty sound. "Well, being late to work on your first day is cruel and unusual. Please get up—and pull your hair back off your face. You don't want to get hair in anybody's ice cream. That would *also* be cruel and unusual."

"I'm up, I'm up," I said. After my shower I quickly made two long braids in my hair and then pulled them back with a ponytail holder. Mom's advice was usually annoying, but she was right about the hair. Nobody wants an ice cream sundae with rainbow sprinkles and Tamiko DNA. Yuck! With a little extra hustle I was able to arrive right on time for our first shift.

After we all hugged hello, we heard a shuffle near the back door. It was Mrs. S., walking in with a tub of ice cream almost bigger than she was.

"Can you girls please help me bring in the ice cream from the van out back?" she asked. "We sold out of seven flavors yesterday!"

The three of us looked at one another. I guess it was time to, you know, work.

"I should have refilled the flavors last night, but I was just too tired," Mrs. S. continued, and then she turned to Allie. "Your dad was nice enough to bring them over to me today."

Right, Allie's dad. The weird thing about Allie's parents was that they always used to fight when they were married. Not like huge blowout fights but lots of little fights, which made us all squirm. They bickered in front of Allie and her little brother, Tanner, and even in front of Sierra and me. I'm pretty sure you're not supposed to fight in front of your daughter's friends, but we *did* go over to their house a lot, I guess. Nobody was really surprised when they got divorced, except for Allie. It's always different when it's your parents. But now that they were divorced, it was like they were best friends or something. They were super-smiley and helpful to each other. They probably got along better than my own parents, even.

We followed Allie's mom through the back door to the minivan that she used to haul stuff back and forth to the shop. She rented a space in an industrial kitchen somewhere else in Bayville, where she made the ice cream and stored it in a big Deepfreeze. Allie's dad was there now too, unloading the tubs, and Tanner was helping him—or doing Tanner's version of helping, which is to say, he watched us doing everything and complained that it was too hot outside.

"Hey, Mr. S.!" I said. "Hi, Tanner."

Before I could get another word in, Allie's mom took one of the tubs from Mr. S. "Enough talking!" she said. "We don't want the ice cream to melt."

"You heard the boss!" Mr. S. said, and we all laughed. Allie and Sierra grabbed buckets, and we lugged them through the back office and into the front parlor. I dumped the bucket into the bin marked VANILLA in one of the shop's long freezers. A curved glass top was open in the back so that we could scoop, but the glass protected the ice cream in the front from sneezing customers and little kids with icky hands. Besides vanilla, chocolate, and strawberry, Mrs. S. had concocted some truly special and delicious flavors, like Lemon Blueberry, Banana Pudding, Butterscotch Chocolate Chunk, and Maple Bacon.

"There's so much more vanilla than anything else," I said, looking at all the flavors lined up.

"It's Mom's best-selling flavor," Allie said.

"Really? Why would anyone get vanilla when there are so many cool things to try?" I asked.

"You know, I think part of the reason is that even the basic flavors are amazing," Allie said. "Mom's vanilla is the best vanilla around."

"It is definitely the most vanilla-y," Sierra chimed in. "I love it!"

"Vanilla-y! Is that even a word?" I teased.

"But also I think people just order the same thing out of habit," Allie went on.

"Well, they can eat as much vanilla as they like, as far as I'm concerned," Mrs. S. said, entering the parlor with a tub of ice cream. "They're still giving me business."

"I guess," I said. "But I love all of the exciting flavors. Do you have any new ones coming out soon?"

"I'm trying a new recipe with lavender, but I'm not sure what other flavors to pair with it," she replied. "I don't want it to be too flowery."

"Ooh, will it be purple? That is an awesome color for ice cream," I said, thinking about all of the cool stories people would post with purple ice cream in the frames.

She smiled. "I could definitely make it purple. Hmm. Maybe Lavender Blackberry?"

Then she turned to Allie. "I've got a bunch of

ordering and bookkeeping to catch up on, so I'm going to leave you girls out front. You're in charge, Allie. You know what to do to set up. The afternoon rush will start soon!"

Allie nodded. "We got this!"

Mrs. S. disappeared into the back, and Allie faced us. She had a serious look on her face.

"Okay, here's the plan," she said. "Sierra, you're on the cash register because you're the best with numbers out of all of us."

Sierra gave a goofy salute. "I will make the mathletes proud!" she said.

"Tamiko, since you're such a great people person, you can take the orders," Allie went on. "I'll fill them, and then you can hand them to the customer."

"People person?" I asked. "You mean like a game show host? I can do that." I held up a scooper like a microphone. *"All right, customer seventy-seven, it's time to play Hoop the Scoop!"* I announced, and then pretended to bounce an invisible basketball around on the counter.

"Tamiko! Watch out!" Sierra scolded.

I looked over. The jar with candy buttons was wobbling. I'd almost knocked into it.

"A shaky landing for star people person Tamiko Sato," I hissed in a sports announcer voice, but Allie just sighed.

"Watch out, Ms. People Person," Allie said. "Or else you'll be the one cleaning the entire shop tonight."

"You wouldn't," I said menacingly.

"I so would," Allie said, but this time she was laughing.

Then the three of us cracked up. We actually did have to clean the store—wiping down the counters and tables, sweeping up, and washing out all the scoops—but Mrs. S. had a service come in and do the hard scrubbing, thank goodness.

"All right," Allie said once we caught our breath. "Can you guys help me get more spoons out of the storage room? And napkins. We need to refill the napkin dispensers too. And make sure all the ice cream cups are stacked up and ready."

After refilling one set of supplies, I took my phone out of my pocket.

"I'm going to take some photos and post them," I said. "You know, just to remind people that Sunday is a great day to come out for ice cream."

8

I dimmed the lights just a *little* to take the perfect snap.

"Okay. Sierra and I can handle the rest of the stuff, I guess," Allie said, but the way she said it, there was an edge in her voice.

Hmm. That was weird. Allie rarely had an attitude. The only time I'd really seen her get mad was when her parents got divorced and told her that she'd be moving and starting school in a new town. And to be honest that was totally understandable, because I'd be really mad about that too. But why was she annoyed now?

I wondered if I should tell her that good marketing is important for any business. I knew that because my brother, Kai, took marketing classes at the high school, and sometimes I helped him study by holding up his flash cards while I painted my nails.

Then I reminded myself that Allie probably wasn't actually mad. Maybe she was just trying to manage Sierra and get everything perfect for our first official day at work. Sierra was my other best friend, but she got distracted a lot and wasn't the most detail-oriented person. Plus she always took on too many things at once. We tried to help her, but sometimes things were a mess. I think Allie and I were both a little nervous about her dropping some ice cream or ringing up someone for five thousand dollars' worth of ice cream by accident.

Still, things were a little different now that Allie went to another school. When we used to see each other every day, we didn't seem to have any problems, but now that we saw her only one or two times a week, things were different. She was still my best friend, but I didn't know every detail of what was going on with her anymore.

I started snapping photos. First I took a picture of the menu sign where the flavors were written in colored chalk. I typed in the caption, Sprinkle Sundays squad goals: try a new flavor at Molly's #IceCream #Bayville #Yum, making sure to throw in some hashtags so people knew how to find the store.

Then I started snapping photos of the shop. It was *so* gorgeous that sometimes I wished I could live there. I took a photo of the vintage metal letters behind the freezers, with light bulbs in them that spelled out ICE CREAM. Then I got a wide shot of the parlor, with the cool black-and-white checkered floor flecked with gold; the high counter with stools looking out the window; and the three round, white tables surrounded by wire chairs. The chair cushions had blue- and cream-colored stripes, which matched the awning on the outside of the building.

There was so much to photograph! Above the register, light fixtures that looked like ice cream cones hung down from the ceiling. So cute! Then I moved on to the buckets inside the counter that held all of the toppings that customers could choose to put on their ice cream or have mixed in. I got a close-up of a bin of rainbow sprinkles, and then a jar of red and yellow and green gummy bears, and another one of some glistening blue gummy fish.

Then I grabbed Allie and Sierra and pulled us all together.

"Sprinkles selfie!" I cried, and I held out the phone and clicked.

"Let me see that before you post it!" Sierra said, grabbing the phone from me.

"Don't worry. You look gorgeous," I said, and I wasn't wrong. Sierra had an amazing smile.

I handed the phone to Sierra so that she could see.

"It's not *bad*," Sierra said, looking at it. "Just don't tag me." Then she continued scrolling through the photo feed on my phone. "Oh my gosh, I can't believe that outfit Jenna wore on Wednesday."

"I know! She looked stunning," I agreed.

"Jenna Robinson?" Allie said. "I thought she always wears jeans and sneakers."

"No, Jenna Horowitz," I corrected her. "Remember her? She was in my fifth-grade class."

Allie shrugged. "So, what was she wearing?"

"A black miniskirt and a long-sleeved white shirt with a collar, and black ankle boots," Sierra reported. "It was so sophisticated!"

"Well, she did copy the whole outfit from the fall cover of *Teen Trend* magazine, so minus ten points for being unoriginal," I pointed out. "But only Jenna would have the guts to wear it, so ten points added."

I liked to pretend to score people's outfits, almost like I really *was* a TV show host.

"Speaking of guts, did you read that chapter about the digestive system in biology?" Sierra asked. "That was so gross. But Mr. Bongort made it really funny, thank goodness."

"Yeah, he was joking around the whole time," I replied. "Cole was picked to reenact the bathroom bit in class," I added for Allie's benefit. "It was hysterical."

"Cole is so annoying," Sierra said. "But it was pretty funny, watching him not be able to find a bathroom fast enough!"

"Well, I wouldn't know," Allie chimed in, and there was that edge to her voice again.

Sierra and I exchanged looks. It was really hard for Allie when she felt left out.

Allie, Sierra, and I used to all go to school together, from kindergarten all the way through sixth grade.

"Well, Mr. Bongort is our science teacher. He's very funny, and nice, too," I told Allie. "And he lets us have five minutes of free time every day, and he wears zebra-print ties to school. I bet he eats a lot of ice cream. I should tell him about this place."

"I need to get more spoons," Allie said in a flat voice, and she left us.

Sierra's eyes followed her. Then she walked over to me.

"Maybe we should stop talking about school stuff," Sierra said. "You know it really hurts Allie that she can't go to school with us."

I sighed.

"First of all, Allie's school is way cooler than MLK, so I don't know what she's complaining about," I said. "She's always sending us bragging pics about Vista Green. How the lunch is like something from a gourmet café, and their computer lab is like something you'd see at NASA."

"I guess you have a point, but I don't want to see her hurt," Sierra admitted.

I wasn't done. "And second of all, what is wrong with us talking about what happens at MLK? School is our life right now. Am I supposed to not talk about my life?" I asked.

Sierra frowned. "I know, but—"

Allie came back into the room then, and Sierra and I clammed up. The little bell on the door jingled as two high-school-aged boys walked into the shop.

I looked at my best friends. Ready or not, it was time to sell some ice cream!

CHAPTER TWO
HAVE YOUR SPRINKLE OF HAPPY!

"I'll have a small vanilla cone, please," one of the boys said.

Vanilla cone? I rolled my eyes. "Are you sure you can stand the excitement?" I asked him.

"Excitement?" he repeated, confused.

I tried another angle. "Our vanilla is really good, but you ought to try another flavor." I then glanced over to a cup of spoons behind the counter. Then I got an idea. "Can I give you a free sample of my favorite? It's called Hokey Pokey, and has bits of honeycomb toffee in it. Mrs. S., who owns the store, says she got the idea for the flavor from an article she read about ice cream in New Zealand, and we're the only shop around that sells it."

The boy shrugged. "Sure," he said.

I gave him a heaping spoonful of Hokey Pokey, making sure to include a super-big piece of toffee in it. I could feel Allie's eyes on me when I handed it to him. I wanted to beam. *Look at how good I am at marketing!* I thought.

The sample was so big and tasty that it took him two bites to try it all.

"This is delicious!" he said. "Okay, one Hokey Pokey scoop in a cone, please."

It was razzle-dazzle time!

"I'm supposed to ask you if you want a waffle cone or a chocolate-dipped cone or a deluxe chocolate-nut-dipped cone," I told him. "But I'm guessing you want a plain, boring old sugar cone?"

He looked to the cones on top of the counter that we used for display. "Okay, ice cream expert. What do you suggest?" he asked.

"With this flavor? We have a caramel-dipped cone that's perfect," I said.

I grabbed the cone for him and announced the order to Sierra, who already had it punched into the register.

When he left, Allie turned to me.

"Tamiko, you can't give out samples that big,"

she said matter-of-factly. "What if he hadn't ordered that flavor? Then we would have been short, and that wouldn't be good for my mom's inventory."

"Yeah, but he *did* order it, so there's no problem," I said. "It's good marketing. Next time he's going to try another new flavor, and then another."

Allie sighed. "I hope so," she responded. We looked up. There wasn't much time to say anything else—the bell jingled again and a line started to form.

After giving cones to an elderly couple, two dads and their kids, a babysitter and a little girl, and a couple of other teenagers, I started to feel tired. It was only one thirty, and the after-lunch crowd was slamming us hard. It was still really hot out, even though it was fall, and everyone wanted ice cream. Each chair had a person in it, and the long line of customers had almost reached the door.

"I'll have a medium cup of the Kitchen Sink, please, with chocolate sauce and a cherry," said the next customer, squinting at the menu above us.

That was the first interesting order I'd taken all day. The Kitchen Sink had a classic vanilla ice cream base, but it was also loaded with crumbled pretzels, potato chips, fudge, and caramel. "Five points for originality!" I cheered, and Sierra laughed.

The woman smiled. "I'm not sure what I did to deserve that, but I'll take it," she said.

The next few orders were not as interesting. Two vanilla cones. One chocolate shake. One chocolate cone. I wanted to offer Strawberry Shortcake or Hokey Pokey samples, but I was worried what Allie might say.

Then a woman came up to the counter wearing pink nursing scrubs. She looked tired, like she had just come off a long shift, maybe. I guessed that she had come to Molly's to add a little bit of happiness to her day.

"Hello. How can I help you?" I asked in my most cheerful customer-service voice.

"I'll just have a little strawberry ice cream in a cup," she said.

How disappointing! I thought. Was that the best she could do? Was she just ordering the strawberry ice cream because it was a habit? Or maybe she wanted to match her scrubs? Was pink her favorite color, and she always ordered her ice cream to match? I looked at her face carefully and noticed there was a unicorn barrette in her hair. Maybe she was a pediatric nurse, or she just liked unicorns.

Then I remembered a photo that my friend MacKenzie had sent me. "Hold on," I said, and took my gloves off. I quickly scrolled through my phone and brought up the pic.

"If you want, I can whip up *this*," I said, and held up the phone. The picture showed a unicorn sundae. There were lots of ways to make them, but this one had pink and blue ice cream topped with mini-marshmallows, whipped cream, and rainbow sprinkles. The mini-marshmallows looked like unicorn ears, and three mini-marshmallows were stacked high for the horn.

The woman's eyes got wide.

"That's very pretty," she said. "But I don't know if I could eat all that."

"Of course you can!" I said. "It's a unicorn sundae, a special treat for a special person. And that person is you."

The woman scrunched up her face, thinking. "Weeeellllll . . ."

Allie spoke up behind me. "Tamiko, I've got the next milkshake ready. And no cell phones while you're serving customers."

I ignored her, because I could see that I almost had this woman convinced.

"You're obviously a hardworking woman," I said. "Don't you deserve a special treat? Something happy to brighten up your day? Since you spend time brightening up everyone else's."

That did it. The woman smiled. "Yes, exactly!" she said. "It's been a rough week. One unicorn sundae, please."

A few people in line behind her laughed and applauded.

"One unicorn sundae, coming right up," I said. I took the milkshake from Allie.

"How exactly am I supposed to make that?" she hissed at me.

"One scoop of strawberry, one scoop of Lemon Blueberry, topped with mini-marshmallows, whipped cream, and rainbow sprinkles," I said, showing her the photo. "We can charge her the medium sundae price."

Allie's eyes brightened a little when she realized this. A medium sundae cost more than twice as much as a single scoop, which meant more profits for her mom's shop.

I delivered the milkshake to its owner and turned back to the line, where a dad with two little girls was waiting.

"What can I get for you?" I asked.

"Well, we were just going to get cones, but I think now we'll get three unicorn sundaes," he said.

"Yay!" the little girls cheered.

"You got it," I said, and I turned back to Allie. She was just starting to put the toppings on the first unicorn sundae.

"We need three more," I told her, and now her eyes got wide with fear. "Let me know if you need help."

But Allie was a trooper. She nodded gratefully. "Thanks, but I think I've got it."

Allie added the mini-marshmallows and whipped cream to the first sundae and topped it off with a flourish of multicolored sprinkles.

"Perfect!" I said. I took it from her and handed it to the nurse. "Have your sprinkle of happy!" I said, and she smiled at me.

"You too!"

Now Allie was working on the three unicorn sundaes. I glanced at the line and saw that it was stretching out the door at this point. Awesome for the shop, but not so awesome for me and Allie!

I took the next order. "One vanilla cone with chocolate sprinkles, one cup of chocolate ice cream," I told Allie.

Then I gave the finished sundaes to the dad with the little girls. "Have your sprinkle of happy!" I repeated, and I heard a lady in line say, "Oh, the girls who work here are just so sweet!"

Maybe we were *too* sweet, because the next four orders were all unicorn sundaes! I saw some of the customers snapping photos of the first ones we had already made.

"We need to keep up!" I urged Allie. "Let me help you with those."

"I got this," she said, scooping out the ice cream into four cups.

I started topping the sundaes with the mini-marshmallows. Allie wiped her hands on her apron.

"I can finish topping," she said. "Go take the next order."

"You got it, boss," I said, and then I turned to help a mom with two little boys who were running around her in circles and screaming. "Chocolate peanut butter! Chocolate peanut butter! Yum!"

"Chocolate peanut butter what?" I asked.

Then I heard Allie's voice behind me. "Four unicorns ready!"

I spun around, and she thrust two sundaes into my hands. I handed them over to the customers, and then when I spun around again, Allie thrust two more into my hands. But I didn't get a good grip on one of them, and it fell to the floor with a sickening *plop!* *Oh, no,* I thought. *Why did this have to happen now? Allie was already a little annoyed at me today.* A couple of customers in line gasped. I decided to try to make a joke out of the situation.

"Unicorn down!" I yelled, and the customers in line laughed. So did Sierra. But Allie wasn't laughing at all. In fact, she was frowning.

"I'll get the mop," Sierra said quickly, and she dashed off while Allie went to work on making a replacement sundae. Her mouth was a thin line.

Honestly, I did not understand why Allie was so upset. It was just one sundae—a sundae that the shop would not have sold if I had not been inspired to convince the nurse to order one. Now we had a shop full of people ordering expensive sundaes instead of plain cups of ice cream. So we lost one—big deal! Hadn't I been making extra money for the shop all day? She should be thanking me instead of giving me dirty looks.

Allie finished the new sundae and handed it to me.

"Be careful with this one," she said.

I rolled my eyes at her. But when I faced the customer, I made sure to have a big smile on my face.

"Here's your sprinkle of happy!" I said, smiling big.

CHAPTER THREE

WHAT IS ALLIE'S DEAL?

"What gave you the idea for the unicorn sundaes?" Allie asked me when we finally had a lull in customers.

It was almost five o'clock, our end-of-shift time. We had been cranking out unicorn sundaes like crazy for almost two hours, and then business had slowly died down. We were wiping the tables, and cleaning the ice cream drips on the freezer, and crushing cookies for the toppings.

"MacKenzie found them online," I replied. "They're trending. And I just had a hunch that that nurse would go for one."

I watched Allie's face carefully when I mentioned MacKenzie. Kenz (what I mostly called her) was a new student at MLK Middle School. Sierra and I had made friends with her because we'd been thinking of Allie and how hard it must be to be the new kid in school. But Allie had been kind of jealous of MacKenzie at first.

"It *is* a good idea," Allie replied after a moment, and she seemed to be cool with the fact that it had come from MacKenzie.

Mrs. S. came out of the back room, stretching.

"I thought I'd leave hours of paperwork behind me when I stopped working for your dad's company, Allie," she said. "But there's a lot more than I bargained for, running this shop. Making the ice cream is the best part."

"Mrs. S., if you're still filling out orders, you might want to order some more mini-marshmallows," I said. "We're low."

She frowned, puzzled. "But I just bought some. They don't usually run out so fast."

I showed her the picture of a unicorn sundae on my phone. "That was before we started selling unicorn sundaes. They're very popular now. You might want to get them on the menu board."

"So that's what all the fuss was I heard out here," Mrs. S. said. "What kind of ice cream did you use?"

26

Allie answered. "The strawberry and the Lemon Blueberry," she replied. "People really seemed to like them. I can show you how to make one."

"Thanks, but not right now," Mrs. S. said. "The girls' moms will be here soon, and, Allie, your dad is on his way with Tanner."

"But I could stay and help you," Allie said. "There's a lot of cleanup to do, and you're going to get an after-dinner rush."

Mrs. S. hugged her. "I've got it, Allie. Don't worry. I'm going to handle the after-dinner crowd and close around seven. It won't be too busy on a Sunday night. You need time to relax before school tomorrow. Plus your dad has a special dinner planned for you and Tanner."

Allie nodded, but I thought she looked a little sad. I tried to imagine what life would be like if I had to spend one weekend with my dad and another with my mom. Getting a break from Mom didn't seem so bad, but like I said before, it's always different when it's your parents.

Mrs. S. put on an apron. "Sierra, can you please cash out for me before you go?"

"Sure thing," Sierra replied, and she started pressing

some buttons on the computerized cash register.

"Thanks so much, girls," Mrs. S. said. "I'm going to get some more stuff from the supply cabinet before you go. Call me when you cash out, Sierra, so I can pay you all for today. And don't forget to split your tips."

"Can you count the tips, Tamiko?" Sierra asked, nodding to the tip jar next to the register.

"Absolutely," I said. I brought the jar to one of the tables and dumped it out. Dollar bills spilled out, along with coins, which started rolling all over the checkered floor.

"Whoops!" I cried, and scrambled to pick them up. I didn't want to lose any of our tip money!

I gathered up the coins and divided them into piles. It was taking forever! While I was still counting, Sierra spoke up.

"The register's a little short," she said. "I'm off by ninety-seven cents."

"That's not a big deal," I said.

Allie, who was wiping off the counter, stopped. "'Not a big deal?'" she repeated. "Don't you realize that all these things add up? Like dropping ice cream onto the floor, and giving huge samples, and now coming up short on the register? This is a real business, you know. It's not a game or a silly MLK homework assignment!"

I looked at Sierra, and her eyes were as wide as mine. Was Allie really freaking out over one dropped sundae and ninety-seven cents? Didn't she realize that I had been helping her mom do more business by up-selling product all day?

"Jeez, Allie. If I wanted to get yelled at, I would have stayed at home so that my mom could yell at me," I said. "I'll pay for the sundae that I dropped. Even though *you* were the one passing it to me too fast."

"What? I did not!" Allie snapped.

"And you can take a dollar out of my tips," Sierra said. "I probably charged someone for a small cone instead of a medium, or something like that. It was such a crazy day, and I was nervous about keeping up. I didn't mean to. I'm sorry, *chica*. We all want to make this work for your mom."

Allie's face softened then. Sierra was always a lot more understanding than I was. Me, I was pretty blunt. But Sierra always seemed to know just how to say things.

29

"Listen, I'm sorry. I didn't mean to yell," Allie said. "Don't worry about it, okay?"

Sierra and I didn't say anything for a few seconds.

"You want me to see if my dad will take us all out for pizza or something?" Allie asked.

I genuinely believed that Allie felt bad. But I felt like I had been stung by a bee, and now there was a tiny painful spot that I couldn't ignore.

"Well, maybe some other time," I said. "I mean, our moms are already on the way. Plus your mom said that your dad had something special planned."

"Right," Allie said. "Maybe next Sunday. We can plan it in advance."

"That's a great idea," Sierra said.

I quickly finished counting the tips in silence. Then I handed out the cash to everyone.

"We each made fourteen dollars and thirty-two cents in tips," I said. "But I'm putting six dollars of mine back into the register to cover the sundae."

I waited for Allie to say, "No, don't worry about it. It was an accident," but she didn't. She nodded at me like that was what I was supposed to do. And then that little painful spot flared up again. Why did Allie have to be so mean?

"Here's my dollar," Sierra said, adding a bill from her tip money to the register. "You can keep the extra three cents."

Allie's face was red now, like she felt awkward about the whole thing. But she didn't stop Sierra from returning the money either.

Mrs. S. returned from the back room. "All done, Sierra?" she asked.

"All ready for you," Sierra replied.

Allie's mom opened the cash register and gave us each the hourly pay that we'd earned, on top of our tips. It took away some of the sting of having to pay for the dropped sundae, but not the sting from feeling slighted by one of my best friends in the world.

"One step closer to my mini-moto," I said, carefully placing the money into my purse. Last Christmas break I'd visited my cousin Hayato in Japan, and he'd had this cool tiny moped that we'd all taken turns on. I'd wanted one of my own for months now, even though Mom had said, *You'll ride one over my dead body.* I'd told her that I would need a ramp to do that, since, you know, I'd be on a moped. She hadn't laughed. Still I kept thinking that if I paid for it, she wouldn't be able to say no.

Sierra motioned to me. "Want to wait outside for our rides?" she asked.

"Sure," I said. "So long, Sprinkle Sundays sisters! See you next Sunday!"

"Thanks, girls!" Mrs. S. called after us. Allie just waved.

We stepped outside.

"Well, that was awkward," Sierra said. "Sorry. I just had to get out of there."

"What is up with Allie?" I asked. "She used to be so chill. But this whole uptight-boss-lady act is not working for me."

"Well, she's going through a lot," Sierra pointed out. "You saw her face when her mom said she couldn't stay at the shop longer."

"I guess," I said. "But that's between her and her parents. She shouldn't be yelling at *us*. We're her friends!"

Sierra just shrugged.

Then my mom's white SUV pulled up, and I flashed Sierra a peace sign.

"Later," I said.

It was only when I climbed into the passenger seat that I realized that while I had sold a bunch of unicorn sundaes, I had not even tried one! What was the point of working in an ice cream shop if you didn't get to stuff your face with ice cream?

I put on my seat belt.

"No sprinkle of happy for me today!" I said, and sighed.

CHAPTER FOUR
FAMILY NIGHT

"No sprinkle of happy?" Mom asked. "Is this job too much for you, Tamiko?"

Ugh. This was why I shouldn't have said anything out loud. My mom *loved* to talk about everything— and I mean everything.

"No, no, no," I said quickly. "It's not too much. But you know, it's work. Work isn't always fun."

"No," she agreed. "That's why it's called work. But I hope that when you grow up, you'll be able to do work that you love. Then it won't feel as hard." She glanced over at me and smiled. "Like maybe you could become a professional toilet seat customizer."

"Why, yes," I said, playing along. "I was thinking of majoring in that in college at Toilet Customization

School. It's really far away, so you won't be able to visit."

"Seriously, Tamiko, I don't like you staying up so late," Mom said. "I got up to use the bathroom at one o'clock, and I saw the light still on under your door."

"When the muse strikes, I must listen," I said.

"I did not know there was a toilet seat muse," Mom replied. "Interesting."

But then she let it drop.

"What's for dinner?" I asked as we pulled into the driveway.

"Dad made hiyashi chuka, since it was so hot out today," Mom replied. Hiyashi chuka was one of my favorite foods, so I heard my stomach rumble and get excited. It was a cold noodle dish made with ramen noodles, but these were nothing like the super-salty ramen sold in those little dehydrated packets. Ramen was just a kind of noodle, and hiyashi chuka was cold ramen with a soy or sesame sauce dressing topped with stuff like cucumbers, ham, and cooked egg. Me? I was a vegetarian by choice, so I usually went for tofu instead of ham. The hiyashi chuka smelled really, really good. "The game just started, so I'll put on the TV in the kitchen when we get inside."

"The game!" I cried. "I almost forgot!"

I belonged to a family of baseball fanatics. We all loved the game—except for Kai. Sometimes Kai was kind of like an odd duckling at our house. We would watch almost any major-league game that came on TV, and because there was no big-league team in our state, we were a house divided. A few years ago Mom's and Dad's favorite teams faced each other in the post-season, and when Mom's team won, Dad didn't say a word in the house for a whole thirty-seven hours. I knew because I counted the hours. Actually, it was thirty-six and a half hours, but I liked to round up.

Today their favorite teams weren't playing, though, so while everyone was interested, the pressure was off. Which was a good thing, because I'd had kind of a rough day, and I did *not* want to deal with baseball drama.

After we parked the car and I got inside, I took off my shoes in the entryway and started to run for the kitchen, but Mom stopped me with her voice.

"Tamiko! You *must* change into clean clothes! You are not getting chocolate sauce all over my house!"

I looked down at my messy clothes. She was right—there was chocolate sauce all over them, and little bits of sprinkles. Usually I always had a retort at the ready, but with this I couldn't argue, so I darted up the stairs to my room.

We lived in a section of Bayville where the houses were all kind of old. Our house was definitely big enough for four people, but we didn't have an "open concept" like those people on TV house hunting shows were always talking about. There was just a living room, no family room. And no man cave in the basement, just a laundry room, although Mom kept threatening to build a "she shed" in the back. Yes, apparently that was a thing—but I think only Mom knew about it.

The one good thing about old houses was that they could have odd layouts, and my house definitely did. My room had a smaller room attached to it. It was never meant to be a walk-in closet (another thing people on TV always wanted), because it had windows, so I don't know what it was originally used for. The windows looked out into the vegetable garden in the backyard and got great light.

I guess most people would call it a craft or sewing room, but Allie had dubbed it my "DIY room" because she said I was always customizing things. And she was right. I didn't usually create things from scratch, like knitting a sweater out of yarn. But I would take a sweater that I was tired of and take off the sleeves, or change out the buttons, or sew cute flower patches onto it, or dye it fuchsia. That was "Doing It Yourself," or, as I liked to think of it, *improving* something.

My parents were okay with me customizing everything, as long as I kept things neat. I did not believe that I was a neat person by nature, but my parents were, and I had to play by their rules at this stage in my life, so there was not much else I could do. Also, when I kept things neat, it was easier to talk Mom into buying me extra glue sticks and glitter.

I was really proud of my DIY room. The storage centerpiece was something I'd customized myself. Mom and Dad had been getting rid of an old hutch they'd had for years—a tall wood cabinet with shelves inside, and doors that swung open. They were going to put it out on the curb, but I convinced them to give it to me. I had seen a hutch like that online, and I remembered how to turn it into a supercute craft closet.

First I painted it. That was during my turquoise phase, so it was turquoise with white trim. Then I bought four white-coated wire racks that were meant for kitchen spices, but were also perfect for paint, glitter jars, and other stuff. Those I attached to the inside of the doors. (Kai "helped" me with the screwdriver and hammer bits. I was really good at using them myself, but Mom insisted that I have supervision. It was kind of funny, because Kai didn't even know how to use them, but he would sit there and watch, which seemed to make Mom happy.)

Finally, I got some cheap plastic bins to put on the shelves to hold other supplies. I jammed a lot of stuff into the hutch. And when I wasn't customizing, I just closed the doors, and my DIY room looked super-neat.

The room also had a big, metal folding table that I'd picked up from the curb and snuck into the house, because the idea of me bringing "trash" into the house grossed my parents out. But I'd cleaned it with that spray that kills 99 percent of germs. On top of the table sat a sewing machine that used to be my grandmother's. It wasn't one of those fancy computerized ones that they make nowadays, but it was easy to use and allowed me to customize my clothes easily. Plus, it was pink.

Mom had given me an extra chair from the basement, and for my last birthday she got me the magnifying desk lamp that I'd asked for. That allowed me to stay up late working on stuff, but I don't think she realized that at the time.

Every time I entered my bedroom, I glanced into my customization area, because just looking at it made me happy. Usually I would go pick up the projects I was working on to see if paint had dried, or glue had set, but today was baseball day, and there was no time.

I put on my good-luck jersey and a clean pair of skinny jeans and jogged down into the kitchen. The game had started, and Mom, Dad, and Kai were seated at the table.

"Are they home or away?" I asked.

"Home," Mom said. "First batter struck out already."

"Yes!" I cheered, and slid into my seat. Then I patiently waited for Mom to put some hiyashi chuka onto my plate.

We didn't eat Japanese food at every single meal. My dad had been born in Tokyo and had come to America to go to school, where he'd met my mom. My mom had been born here and had grown up just a few hours from Bayville. So she liked to mostly eat and cook American food, but my dad missed the food that he'd grown up with. When he cooked, we usually ate food that he loved.

Sometimes when I thought about my parents, I got really happy. They just *worked* together. It made me kind of sad to think about Allie's parents being divorced now. I didn't know what I would do if my parents got divorced. I'd definitely want to live with Dad, that's for sure—*he'd* never shake me out of bed— but if I lived only with Dad, who once wore one black shoe and one brown shoe to work when Mom was away, would I ever get out of bed? Would Kai and I live in the same house, like Allie and Tanner? Would the family ever have game day again?

I guess I was lost in thought, because Dad prodded my elbow.

"How was your shift at the ice cream shop, Tamiko?" he asked, picking up some noodles with his chopsticks.

"She wasn't happy," Mom answered for me.

"I was *mostly* happy," I countered. "Things just got a little tense with Allie at the end."

"Then maybe you should forget this idea," Mom

said. "You already have a very busy schedule, Tamiko."

"Well, I think Tamiko's having a job at this age is a good way to build character," Dad said. "But maybe your mom is right. You shouldn't do too much."

"I'm *not* doing too much," I assured them. "My only other extracurricular right now is cross-country, and that's only on Tuesdays, Thursdays, and Saturday mornings. And I've been getting good grades. I still have plenty of time to do homework."

"That is true," Dad said. "I check your grades every night. They are excellent."

I smiled at him, and he winked. All of my grades were really good except for gym, which wasn't *bad*, but Mom would definitely be mad. But let's be real. Get sweaty enough to have to shower in the locker room? I did so much exercise during the week, it wasn't like I was slacking. I just would rather not shower in that gross school water that kind of smelled like the sewer. Of course, I was sure that *Allie's* super-cool Vista Green locker room was state-of-the-art and birds sang or something when you stepped inside, and the water smelled like delicate lavender. I rolled my eyes at the thought.

Kai chimed in. "You might not have to worry

about that ice cream shop being around for long, anyway," he said. He scrolled through his phone. "The shop is practically invisible on social media. Who do you serve ice cream to? Old people?"

"Kai, no phone at the table, please," Mom said. She shook her head. "How many times . . ."

"That's not nice, Kai," I said. "But then again, you're kind of right. I have been bugging Mrs. S. to set up a website. Or a SuperSnap. Or *anything*. I've been posting for the shop, but I'm using my account."

"She needs to do all those things, or she'll sink," Kai said. "Not to mention all of the print opportunities in a small town like this. She could be getting free press from the *Bayville Gazette*."

"Allie got an article in her school newspaper," I said.

"That's a start," Kai said. "You know, I should give Mrs. S. a hand with this. I'm going to come up with some ideas for her."

"Go for it," I said. "Coming up with ideas is the easy part. Getting her to do them is the hard part."

"So, why weren't you happy at work today?" Mom asked. She never let anything go.

I sighed. "Listen," I said, "Allie and I used to see each other every day at school. Now practically the only day I get to see her is Sunday. It's just a little weird sometimes. But I like working. When it stops being fun, I'll quit. I promise."

My parents looked at each other. Dad nodded.

"Fine," Mom said.

"And I will keep checking your grades," Dad added.

"That's settled," Mom said. "Now, I want to remind you both that we've got the food festival next Saturday. Tamiko, we're going to have to leave right after your cross-country meet."

A roar went up from the crowd on the TV.

"Home run!" I cheered, jumping up. "But was it our team or the other? I wasn't paying attention. That would be awkward if I were just cheering for the other team."

"Tamiko, settle down, please!" Mom pleaded.

I sat down, and the game went to commercial. *Boring.* For as much as I liked learning about marketing, I couldn't stand commercials. Just get me to the good stuff!

Since Mom had told me to settle down, I glanced around at the clock. It was 6:05 p.m., which meant that it was 8:05 a.m. in Tokyo. And if it was 8:05 a.m. in Tokyo—

"Grandpa's awake!" I yelled, and I jumped up again and made a beeline for my tablet.

Grandpa Sato, my dad's father, called us almost every morning when he woke up. I swiped the screen, and his face popped up. Right on time!

"Ojiichan!" I said, which meant "grandfather" in Japanese. I had been taking Japanese lessons since I was five years old—until I started cross-country this year, and the meets conflicted with the class times. I could speak Japanese pretty well, but I was lucky that Grandpa Sato liked to practice his English when he called us. It was just easier.

"*Ohayo*, Tamiko," he said. (That meant "good morning.") "Are you watching the game?"

"Yes," I replied, glancing at the screen. "We're up two–nothing."

"Very good," Grandpa replied. "The Swallows did very well last night. They won."

Grandpa was a big fan of Nippon Professional Baseball in Japan, or *Puro Yakyū* as it was called over there.

"I read online that Brad Cortland is injured," I told him. Some of the baseball players in Japan were from America.

"Yes, he sprained his knee sliding into second base," Grandpa said, shaking his head. "He is one of their strongest hitters. But they won the game without him anyway."

Mom appeared behind me. "We are just finishing dinner," she said. "Would you like to talk to Toshi now?"

"Yes," Grandpa said with a nod. "Talk to you tomorrow, Tamiko-chan!"

"Bye, *Ojiichan*!" I said with a wave, and then my dad got up from the table and started talking to Grandpa in Japanese.

I sat down at the table. "Only ten more months until we go back," I said with a little bit of a sigh. Every summer we made a trip to Japan to see my grandfather, my aunt and uncle, and my cousins. I absolutely loved it there, especially when we went to Tokyo. Everything in that city was so colorful and bright and inspiring.

As I put another mouthful of noodles into my mouth, Mom glanced at me.

"You're smiling," she said. "It looks like you got your sprinkle of happy today after all."

"Yes, and I'd better enjoy it while I can," I said. "After all, tomorrow is Monday!"

CHAPTER FIVE
PERSPECTIVE

If Sundays were a sprinkle of happy, then Mondays were definitely a dollop of doom. Mondays meant back to school, back to homework, back to waking up even *earlier*—and they also meant going to art class with Mr. Rivera.

You might have thought that art would be my favorite subject in school since I loved DIY and all that jazz, but that was not the case. There were several reasons for that, but the main reason was Mr. Rivera.

An art teacher should be a creative warrior with the heart of a dragon and the soul of a unicorn, right? The kind of teacher who played ukulele and always had a paintbrush behind one ear? That's what you'd think. But Mr. Rivera had the heart of a mouse and the soul of an even more boring mouse—and I didn't like that at all.

Want to know how boring he was? Mr. Rivera always wore a shirt and a tie to school. *A shirt and a tie!* Even the male math teachers didn't wear that. And secondly, he usually wore brown pants, a beige shirt, and a black tie. Blah! No color!

Third of all, he was not a fan of customizing—at all. He just wanted everyone to copy what he did, exactly the way he did it.

Where was the art? The expression? The love for the craft?

Just as an example, the day after the Sprinkle Sundays sisters' first official shift at the ice cream shop, Mr. Rivera announced that the class was going to learn about perspective, which basically meant that you drew things on a flat piece of paper so that they looked 3-D. There was this genius artist I'd seen online who created these amazing chalk drawings in public spaces, so that it looked like there was a shark coming out of the sidewalk, or a deep pool in the middle of a courtyard, and I was really excited to make something that kind of looked like that.

I was so excited for this assignment, I raised my hand.

"Have you seen the work of the guy who does the amazing chalk drawings?" I asked, without waiting for Mr. Rivera to call on me.

"That does not sound familiar, Tamiko," Mr. Rivera said.

"But it's all over social media," I informed him.

"Well, *I* am not all over social media," he replied.

I took my phone out of my backpack. "Here, let me show you!"

"I'm afraid that if you take that phone out of your book bag again, I will have to confiscate it," Mr. Rivera said. "It's against school rules. Right now we're going to begin our lesson."

He walked to the front of the room, to one of those big easels. He turned over a piece of poster board to reveal a large photo of a kitchen. (Side note: according to Allie, every classroom in her school had a wireless projector connected to the teacher's laptop, so all of the lessons were projected onto a screen in front of the class. No more chalkboards, whiteboards, or old-school paper easels. Another reason why it wasn't fair that she got upset when we talked about MLK. Her school was way better!)

"Let's begin by discussing one-point perspective,"

he said. "The surfaces in the photo facing you, the viewer, show their true shape. They are drawn using mostly horizontal and vertical lines. Like this rectangular refrigerator."

He traced a refrigerator with a marker. I'm not joking. A *refrigerator*. By this time I was yawning. He went on to talk about the vanishing point, which was the point right in front of your eyes when you looked at something, and the horizon line, which was at eye level, and then he started drawing a bunch more lines over the photo of the kitchen that, frankly, just left me bored and confused.

He turned over another page on the big easel.

"For our first lesson in perspective, we're going to draw a cube," he said.

"I can hardly stand the excitement," I muttered under my breath. Mr. Rivera didn't hear me, but Ewan Kim was sitting next to me, and he laughed.

So that was what we did in art class. We learned how to draw cubes. I drew several cubes, and then I started customizing them with lightning bolt designs, because I needed *something* interesting in my life.

"Tamiko, please don't add any new lines to your drawing," Mr. Rivera said as he examined my cubes over my shoulder. "This exercise is all about lines."

"Exercise? I thought exercise was for gym class, not art class, and I hate gym class anyway," I wanted to say. But I didn't, because Mr. Rivera would have heard me this time. On my progress report the year before, several teachers had made comments about me "talking out of turn," and Mom and Dad had not been happy.

So, I sadly erased my lightning bolts, but I made sure not to erase them all the way, so that you could still see their little outlines, and when the bell rang, I had created nothing but boring, plain old cubes with sad, shadowy erased lightning bolts underneath.

My next class was English, which I had with my new friend MacKenzie. She was staring at the open book in her hand, making a squinty, frowny face.

"Hey, Kenz!" I greeted her.

She put down the book in frustration. "Oh, hi, Tamiko."

She said it like she was upset about something.

"You okay?" I asked.

"This book is so hard," she complained, nodding toward the novel on her desk, the one we were reading for class. She lowered her voice. "I've got an appointment for testing after school today."

I nodded, because she had explained that things were tricky for her at school. MacKenzie had always had trouble reading, but somehow she'd never been tested for dyslexia when she was younger. I guessed that it must be pretty hard to get through the day if reading was a struggle.

"I can help you with the book at lunch," I said. "Go over all the juicy parts."

She smiled. "Thanks. That would be great. And I need to hear all about what happened at the ice cream shop yesterday."

I realized that I hadn't told MacKenzie how successful the unicorn sundaes had been!

"Definitely," I promised. I decided to keep the news a surprise until lunch, because the bell rang.

"Good morning, class," said Ms. Johnson, our English teacher.

Ms. Johnson was, IMHO, a better teacher than Mr. Rivera. For one thing, she dressed way cooler, accenting her clothing with print scarves and bangles and funky necklaces. She wore her dark hair in, like, a hundred skinny braids and usually kept them tied back, away from her face.

She was also just way more interesting than Mr. Rivera. And I don't mean flashy interesting, like Allie's new English teacher, who started each class with a one-minute disco dance, complete with a disco ball. No, I mean *genuinely* interesting. She had traveled all over the world and had a real-life story to tell us every time we read a new book. And when she talked about books, she really *got* them. And then she made *you* get them.

Ms. Johnson started class by passing out vocabulary worksheets (no laptops at MLK).

"These words are from your novels," she said. "Today I'd like everyone to write a short story using five words from the list."

I scanned the list. One word popped out at me.

"Perspective (n), a point of view on a topic or idea; also, a drawing technique on a two-dimensional surface depicting three-dimensional objects."

I tapped my pen on the desk, something I did when I was thinking. Here was that word again: "perspective." Well, my perspective was that this assignment was going to be a good one.

I finished by the end of class, feeling pretty good about it, and then MacKenzie and I walked to the cafeteria together and I got in line.

I did not love our cafeteria food, but I also didn't hate it. The salad bar was decent, and the greasy veggie burgers on Tuesdays didn't bother me, though they could definitely have been a lot tastier. For the first five years of my school career, Mom had crafted perfect Japanese-style bento box lunches for me every single day, complete with hard-boiled eggs molded into heart and star shapes, and sometimes even a homemade card. Everyone was jealous of me, but it didn't stop me from wanting that French bread pizza they sometimes served on Fridays.

Then one day she just gave up. "I can't do this anymore!" she announced one morning, and handed me a lunch card. And that was it.

Sierra and MacKenzie were both lunch-bringers, so by the time I brought my tray of applesauce, salad, and falafel patty to the table, they were already eating and talking.

I nodded to the other girls at our table—Kyra, Victoria, and Claire—and sat down next to Sierra. MacKenzie looked really happy.

"Sierra was just telling me that the unicorn sundaes were a big hit," she said.

"Hey! I wanted to tell her," I said.

"Sorry," Sierra said with a shrug.

"I'm glad they sold well," MacKenzie said. "They looked so pretty in the picture. I'm going to have to get one on Sunday."

"I hope Mrs. S. puts it on the menu," I said. "She is not always open to new ideas. But she seemed to like that we sold a lot of sundaes."

"I think she *has* to put it on the menu," Sierra said. "I'm sure people will be asking for it again."

"It must be so much fun working there," MacKenzie said.

I looked at Sierra. "Well, *mostly* fun," I said. "I mean, I love Allie, but she is way too uptight working at the shop."

"What do you mean?" MacKenzie asked.

"Well, Tamiko accidentally dropped a sundae," Sierra replied, "and I came up short a dollar on the register. And the samples we gave out were too big."

"And Allie freaked out!" I said. "And when we offered to pay for it out of our wages, she didn't tell us no. I mean, it's not fair! I was up-selling product for her all day. What's one dropped sundae? She just needs to relax."

I was expecting MacKenzie to agree with me, but

55

instead she got a thoughtful look on her face.

"Well, you know that my mom owns a home-made jewelry business, right?" she asked.

I shook my head. "No, I did *not* know that. Why would you keep that a secret? That is so cool."

"Well, she's looking for a place in town to open up a shop, or a shop that will sell her stuff," MacKenzie went on. "For now she's just been selling it online. And I know that every penny counts! She has this computer program that does profit and loss, and she says that even a few cents can make a huge difference, especially at first."

"Really?" I asked.

MacKenzie nodded. "It's one reason why Mom has been able to make a living doing what she loves. Because she's really careful with the money she spends on the business."

"I think Allie tried to tell us the same thing," Sierra said thoughtfully. "I guess we just needed to see things from a different point of view."

There it was. "Perspective!" I said, so loudly that a few kids turned to stare at me. So I lowered my voice.

"What was that about?" Sierra asked, laughing.

"It means that the universe is telling us that we

must forgive Allie and make up with her," I said. I quickly took out my phone. "Sierra, selfie, now!"

I mean, if an emergency selfie didn't defuse any drama, what would? Sierra and I put our heads together. I made my standard selfie face and snapped the photo. Then I added tons of hearts and some text.

WE MISS YOU, ALLIE! XOXO!

Then I sent it to her and stared at my phone.

"What if she's not looking at her phone right now?" Sierra asked. "She might not be able to respond right away."

But she did. Allie sent a photo of herself smiling right back.

I MISS U TOO!

"Done!" I said, and then I gazed up at the ceiling. "Thank you, universe."

My friendship problems were solved. The Sprinkle Sundays sisters were back on track!

CHAPTER SIX
TOO SWEET!

School dragged on pretty slowly that week, but I guess not too slowly, because suddenly it was Saturday. I was in the back seat of the car when I noticed that Mom had turned around and was facing me. And her lips were moving.

With a sigh I took off my headphones.

"Yes?" I asked.

"I was just asking you and Kai if you were excited to be seeing your friends from Japanese school today," she said.

"Mom, you always ask us the same thing," I complained.

Kai's response was much more charming. "Sachi and Mike have been texting about it since last week," he said. "I haven't seen them in months!"

"And I haven't seen Keiko and Ken in months either, so of course I'm excited to see them," I said, and then I put my headphones back on.

It was an hour-and-a-half drive from Bayville to Green Point, the site of the Japanese Cultural Center— the only one in our whole state. My parents had been taking Kai and me to events there since we'd been born, and I honestly loved it there. The center was always having festivals—music festivals, food festivals, holiday festivals—and Japanese Americans from all over our state and beyond would go to them.

Keiko and Ken were my two best Japanese friends. Before I'd started cross-country, we'd all gone to Japanese school together, where we'd learned the language. In fact, Keiko and Ken were the only Japanese American kids I knew well. While MLK was a pretty diverse school, I was the only Japanese kid there. I was friends with a few of the Korean American kids, and the Chinese American kids, and Katie Phan was Vietnamese American, and I was friends with her, too. And while I guessed we had some things in common that I didn't have in common with Sierra and Allie, there was nobody other than me at the school who understood exactly what it was like to be Japanese.

That was why I liked having Keiko and Ken in my life. I was five years old when I met them, when we were little kids running around like maniacs at one of the outdoor festivals. Keiko was chasing me and Ken, and we were trying to hide from her. This freaked out our parents, who thought we were lost, and they were mad at first when they found us. But when they saw how well we were all getting along, they became friends with each other too. And then for every festival after that, Keiko, Ken, and I hung out together, so we were pretty close—as close as you could be without being *best friends*, like me and Allie and Sierra were.

As we got older, we were able to use social media to keep in touch, so we didn't have to wait for festivals to "see" each other. I mostly communicated with Keiko on SuperSnap, because we were both into street fashion and were always exchanging outfit ideas. Keiko had helped me customize a scarf that I'd worn to the Winter Bash the previous year.

While at first I'd been thinking that I might wear something flowy to the festival, I had recently been inspired by photos of girls wearing different kinds of plaid. So I'd chopped off the sleeves of a baggy plaid shirt and now wore it on top of a T-shirt with a *kawaii* (that meant "cute") frog on it. I'd paired that with skinny black jeans and black sneakers. I'd put my hair into a high ponytail and wrapped another scrap of plaid fabric around it.

The parking lot was already very crowded when we pulled in. It was a beautiful day, not too hot and not too cold. Colorful tents dotted the green lawn outside the white, one-story Japanese Cultural Center building.

When I stepped out of the car, a million different delicious smells hit my nose. My stomach rumbled.

"I am soooo hungry!" I said, stretching.

Mom gave me some money. "Get real food," she said. "Not just sweets."

"Thank you," I said, though we both knew I was going to get something yummy and definitely sugary, and then I ran off to find Keiko and Ken. I knew from Keiko's texts that she and Ken had been there for an hour already. I scanned the crowd of mostly Japanese people—but not *all* Japanese people, because all kinds of people will go to a festival when there's really good food—until I spotted an explosion of color and knew it had to be Keiko.

"Keiko!" I yelled.

She spun around. Keiko wore her glossy black hair in a chin-length bob, with perfect bangs. She'd wanted to dye her hair pink for a year now, I knew, but her parents wouldn't let her. But she'd made up for it with a super-colorful outfit. She wore a cute, short-sleeved dress with a bright, cartoony print on it, purple tights, and black boots.

"Tamiko!" She ran toward me, and we hugged. "Love the plaid," she said. "That is very in right now."

"And I love your dress," I replied. "Where did you get it?"

"I found it online," she said. "Used up all my birthday money."

"It is fabulous!" I said. "Spin around!"

She happily did so, and her skirt twirled perfectly. I looked around. "Where's Ken?"

Her cheeks turned a little bit pink. "He's getting me a banana," she said.

"Wait, what?" I asked. "Since when does Ken ever get us stuff?"

Keiko shrugged and looked like she might answer, but then Ken walked up holding two chocolate-and-sprinkle-covered bananas on sticks. He handed one to Keiko.

"Oh, hey, Tamiko," he said

"Hey, Ken," I said. "Chocolate-covered bananas? That's new. Where's mine?"

He nodded. "The guy selling them says he used to sell them at food festivals in Japan." He took a bite. "Pretty good. You should get one."

I noticed that he hadn't offered to get me one, like he'd done with Keiko, and he had ignored my question. I didn't pursue the topic.

"I need to eat some real food first, or Mom will freak," I said. I sniffed the air. "Is that yakitori I smell?"

"You know it is," Keiko said. "Come on. We'll walk with you."

We walked across the grounds toward the yakitori stand, which was easy to spot because of the smoke rising from it. Yakitori was grilled meat on a stick, and it was really yummy, but since I only ate veggies, they had this Americanized version of it made with tempeh, a kind of soy product.

"So, I'm really excited about that new anime dub coming out, *Warrior Spawn*," Keiko said.

I stopped. Anime was what the Japanese called animation, and we did it better than anybody else. All of my favorite cartoon shows were anime. I absolutely loved fantasy anime, stories about magical creatures and mermaid girls and stuff like that, and so did Keiko. Ken had always been a fan of the fighting stuff like *Warrior Spawn*—but Keiko? This caught me off guard.

"Since when do you like that kind of anime?" I asked Keiko.

She blushed a little again and shrugged. "Ken told me about it, and I like it."

Ken smiled at her, and she smiled back. I looked at them. They smiled a *little* too long at each other, almost like they knew something that I didn't. I started to get a weird feeling about them, but I pushed it aside. I was too hungry.

We passed by several food stands on our way to the yakitori tent. There was a booth selling rice balls, of course. And a guy making takoyaki dumplings, which were basically dough balls filled with chopped-up octopus and other stuff and topped with sauce and mayo. I didn't eat them, but Kai loved them. I wondered if he'd bought some dumplings yet.

Then there was a vegetable tempura stand, and a new booth selling something called rice burgers.

I stepped up for a closer look. "Oh my gosh! The buns are made of rice!"

Instead of bread buns, the katsu—a fried chicken cutlet, or a fried tofu option, which they had—was sandwiched inside a bun made of pressed-together rice.

"Hmm, should I try that instead of the yakitori?" I asked.

"Go for it!" Keiko said.

We got in line to order.

"Are you thirsty, Keiko?" Ken asked. "I could go in that other line and get some water."

"No, thanks," Keiko replied.

"Oh, thanks for offering. *I'm* as thirsty as a dog," I said. "Could you please get me some water?"

Ken looked like he was about to say no, but then Keiko gave him a look.

"Sure," he said, and he ran off.

Now was my time to ask Keiko all of the questions.

"All right, missy," I said when Ken was out of ear-shot. "What is going on between you two?"

Keiko blushed again. "It's just, well, we like each other," she said.

"Yeah, I know," I said. "We all like each other."

"No, I mean we *like* each other," she repeated, emphasizing the word "like" this time.

"Like, boyfriend and girlfriend?" I asked. Although

65

it had started to seem kind of obvious, I still did not quite believe what I was hearing.

She shook her head. "No. I mean, our parents won't let us date yet. They say we're too young. But maybe when we're sixteen . . ."

"Oh no!" I said. I knew how this worked. Someone—me—became the third wheel, and I was *not* about that life. "You cannot do this. The three of us are a team. Keiko, Ken, and Tamiko. You can't start messing with the friendship formula. It will ruin everything!"

Keiko frowned. "Don't be like this, Tamiko," she said. "Ken and I can't help it if we like each other that way. Someday you will have someone you like too, and we'll be supportive, no matter who he or she is."

At that moment Ken returned.

"Here you go, Tamiko," he said. Then he gave a bottle of water to Keiko, too. "And I got you one anyway."

"Thanks," she said, smiling at him.

"Ugh! It's a good thing I haven't eaten yet, or I would be *gagging* right now," I said loudly, and a few people in line turned to stare at me.

Now it was Ken's turn to blush.

A few minutes later I had a tofu katsu rice burger with chili sauce in my hand. I ate it standing up as we walked around the festival. I would have enjoyed it more if Ken and Keiko hadn't been looking at each other with dopey eyes the whole time.

"You should get dessert," Keiko said. "That banana was awesome."

"I'm not sure if I want dessert, because it's already too sweet around here," I said, glaring at them. Normally they would have laughed at me for the pun, but they didn't seem to understand that I was insulting them.

But of course I didn't really mean what I said—obviously, I wanted dessert.

"Where's the taiyaki stand?" I asked.

"Over there," Ken said, pointing to the stand with the longest line at the festival.

I was a fiend for taiyaki—a golden brown, doughy pancake-like cake filled with stuff like red bean paste, custard, or sweet potato. What made taiyaki so fun was that it was shaped like a fish. There was no fish in it, though. *Taiyaki* meant "baked fish" in Japanese. As we got in the line, I tried to decide which kind I would get.

Then I saw someone walking by me biting into a taiyaki topped with something that looked like chocolate ice cream! But that couldn't be. Who'd ever heard of taiyaki topped with ice cream?

"Excuse me," I said to the man biting into his cake. "What kind of taiyaki is that?"

"It's red bean on the inside and ice cream on top," he replied.

"Thanks," I said, and I turned to Keiko. "Did you know about this?"

"No," she replied.

"It's all the rage in New York City," Ken said.

"How do you know that?" I asked, and Ken pointed to a sign on the taiyaki booth.

TRY OUR NEW ICE CREAM TAIYAKI!
ALL THE RAGE IN NEW YORK CITY!

Now there was no question about what I would order—red bean taiyaki with ice cream, just like the man had! When I finally got to the front of the line, I ordered a big one. Talk about a fishful of happy!

I could see that two workers were busy behind the order counter. One was pouring the taiyaki batter inside the metal mold to make the cakes. She closed the lid to the mold and placed the mold over an electric burner to cook the cakes inside. Another worker was taking out the finished cakes, slicing into them into buns, filling them with red bean paste, and decorating them with chocolate sauce and candy. I asked if mine could look like that too.

When I got my taiyaki, the cake was still warm and the ice cream was melty but still cold.

"This is the best thing I have ever eaten," I announced.

Ken got one too, and he held it out to Keiko so that she could take a bite.

Ew, I thought. I didn't know how much more of the Keiko-Ken lovefest I could take.

Keiko was just as impressed with the taiyaki.

"If there was a taiyaki shop by me, I'd eat one of these a week," she said.

Then my phone beeped, and I got a text from my mom.

Grandma's here!

"I've got to go see my grandma," I told Keiko and Ken. "Feel free to stop by in a few minutes. I just want to say hi to her alone first."

I jogged off, trying not to think about how gross

the two lovebirds were. Grandma Sasaki—my mom's mom—lived an hour away from the cultural center, but in the opposite direction from us. So when we visited her, it took more than *two hours*. I hated that she lived so far away! But it wasn't as far as Tokyo, so I guess I couldn't complain.

Mom and Grandma were waiting for me by the yakitori stand. Grandma was at least four inches shorter than my mom. I would never tell her this, but I kind of thought she had shrunk. In old pictures she looked like she was taller. She had curly gray hair framing her round face. She was in her early seventies, but she also had more energy than most other people I knew. She loved to wear jogging suits in bright colors, and today she was wearing a bright blue one.

"Grandma, you surprised us!" I cried. "I didn't know you were coming to the festival today."

"I decided at the last minute to take the drive," she replied. "I missed you all." Then she looked around, smiling. "And I also ran out of food in my refrigerator." I laughed at her joke. Grandma's fridge was *always* stocked with the important food groups— like whipped cream and strawberries and everything yummy that you could imagine. She opened her arms and gave me a hug. "My little Tamiko! You grew since I last saw you!"

"I don't think so," I said. "I think my hair is giving me some extra inches today."

"Well, you are as tall as I am now," she said. "And soon you will be taller. Come, show me what's good to eat today!"

She linked her arm with mine, and we walked across the grass. She asked me questions about school, and I asked her how her cat was doing.

"She is always trying to eat my food!" Grandma Sasaki said, and she laughed. "Sometimes I shoo her away. But sometimes I make her a little plate. It makes her so happy."

There were a lot of awesome things about Grandma Sasaki, but the most awesome thing was that she was always smiling, and always positive about things.

"Look at you two!" Grandma said as Keiko and Ken joined us. "Everyone is getting so tall. And, Keiko, I love your colorful dress. Maybe I can borrow it sometime."

Keiko laughed. "Sure, anytime!"

I held out my phone. "Family squad selfie!" I said, and we all gathered around Grandma for a picture.

"You kids and your phones," she said. "You can't live without them."

"Nope," I agreed.

Grandma Sasaki kissed me. "Go have fun with your friends, Tamiko," she said. "I am coming for a long visit to your house soon."

"Yay!" I said, and I hugged her. Then I headed off with Keiko and Ken. We spent the rest of the afternoon tasting more food and walking around, and when we got tired, we hung out under our favorite tree. At around four o'clock I got a text from my mom saying to meet her at the car.

"See you both at the next festival," I said.

Keiko and Ken looked at each other sadly. They lived too far away to see each other in between festivals. So it would be a while before they saw each other again.

"The next festival is, like, six weeks away," Keiko said, making a sad face.

"It will go fast," Ken said.

I rolled my eyes. "Later," I said, and headed to the parking lot.

"Did you have fun?" Mom asked as I walked up to the car.

I nodded. "Sure."

Kai rubbed his belly. "I ate so much! I had two of those ice cream taiyaki. They were awesome!"

"Right?" I said, climbing into the car.

"Somebody should open up a taiyaki shop in Bayville," Kai remarked. "I bet there's a real market for it there."

That was when it hit me. Like a bolt of lightning!

Mrs. S. owned an ice cream shop. She could serve ice cream taiyaki! She'd be the only one doing it for miles and miles!

"Kai, you are a genius," I said.

On the ride home I did something very strange for my standards: I didn't listen to music. I researched the ice cream taiyaki phenomenon on my phone. But I also kept my headphones in my ears, just so that my parents wouldn't bug me (which they did anyway).

When we got home, I started printing out some of the articles I'd found. I couldn't wait for our Sprinkle Sunday the next day.

I just knew that Mrs. S. was going to love my idea!

CHAPTER SEVEN
OR NOT SO MUCH

The next morning I was running around with my paper-clipped printouts about taiyaki when Kai stopped me.

"What is that?" he asked.

"I'm going to tell Mrs. S. that she needs to start serving taiyaki at the shop," I said.

Kai took the papers from me. He put his hand on his chin. "Hmmm."

"Hmmm what?" I asked. "Yesterday you said an ice cream taiyaki shop would do great in this town."

"I did," he admitted. "But you can't just jump into something like this. You need to look at spending trends to find out if it's something the community wants. And you also need to see if you have the right equipment and materials to make this. You also need to do a business plan—profit and loss, expected sales. You can't just hand Mrs. S. a bunch of Internet articles. Look, you're going to need to cite credible sources in your market research, Miko."

I pulled my articles away from Kai. He was such a know-it-all sometimes.

"We can worry about that later," I said. "I just need to convince Mrs. S. that it's a good idea."

Kai shrugged. "Well, if I were making a business pitch, I'd at least put all my papers in a folder or something."

I didn't answer him, but I knew he was right. So I went back to my bedroom. I scrounged up a folder from my craft closet—a pink sparkly one. Then I cut out a photo of a happy-looking woman biting into an ice cream taiyaki and pasted it to the front of the folder. It was perfect!

I was so excited to talk to Mrs. S. that I had Dad drop me off at the store at twelve thirty, fifteen minutes earlier than I needed to be there. When I got in, Allie and Mrs. S. were working behind the counter. I glanced at the menu board and saw UNICORN SUNDAE listed, and I felt like cheering. That was a good sign!

"Hey, Allie! Hey, Mrs. S.!" I said cheerfully.

"Hi, Tamiko," Allie said, handing a milkshake across the counter to a customer.

"Tamiko, it's nice to see you here early," Mrs. S. said. "But you don't have to come here before your shift, you know. I can't pay you for the extra time."

"Don't worry," I said. "I just came to talk to you about something." I held out the folder.

Mrs. S. wiped her hands on a towel and took it from me. "What's this?"

"It's all the rage in New York City," I said. "Taiyaki is a traditional Japanese dessert. It tastes like a pancake. But you can put ice cream on top of it! It would be perfect for the shop!"

Allie walked up to her mom and looked over her shoulder as Mrs. S. flipped through the articles. I tapped my foot with excitement.

"So, the cakes are made to order?" Mrs. S. asked.

"Usually," I replied. "Or the same day, at least. It's best when the cakes are warm."

"That would be impossible!" Allie said, before Mrs. S. could say anything. "You would need an extra person to make the cakes."

"Well, it's just the same as when you do the

76

mix-ins," I said. "Instead of mixing stuff into ice cream, you'd be pouring the batter into the machine. And then you just wait until they're cooked and put ice cream on top. The batter could be made in advance, though."

"The machine is a problem too," Allie said. "First, we don't have one. And I bet it gets really hot, right?"

I nodded.

Allie made a gesture with her hand. "Well, just look around! This is an ice cream shop! Everything has to stay cold."

"But that's not true," I said. "There's hot chocolate sauce that we serve. Plus, the machine doesn't have to be next to the ice cream. Taiyaki is just something to sell that would make a lot of *dough*," I argued, hoping she'd appreciate the pun, but I already knew that Allie was totally against the idea.

"Where would it go? This is a tiny shop," Allie said.

I looked at Mrs. S.

"Allie makes some good points," she said. "And also, it looks like the taiyaki machines are pretty expensive."

"You can get cheap ones online, but if you want

the professional ones, they can be a lot of money," I admitted. "But I was thinking maybe we could save our tips and put them toward a machine! I'd put my tips toward that."

Sierra was walking into the shop.

"Put our tips toward what?" she asked.

"Tamiko has another *Tamiko idea*," Allie said.

Now, that made me angry with Allie all over again. First of all, it was a good idea. And what did she mean by "another Tamiko idea"? The way she'd said it was kind of mean. I would have asked her, but I was still trying to impress Mrs. S.

"I'll think about it," Mrs. S. said, in a tone of voice that meant she was just saying that to be nice. "Thanks for the idea. I always like to think of new things. It's probably not viable now, but you never know about what we can do in the future." My heart sank. She kept the folder at least.

Then she changed the subject. "Tamiko, Allie told me it got a little crazy last week. So maybe you can also make some of the simple orders, like the cups and cones, and leave Allie to the mix-ins, shakes, and sundaes. How does that sound?"

"It sounds great," I said. "I offered to help last

week, but Allie wanted to handle it on her own."

"That's my Allie," Mrs. S. said with a smile. "But I think it will work better with you working as a team, especially during the rush."

I nodded. "Got it!" I glanced at Allie, but she wouldn't meet my eye.

"Great," Mrs. S. said. She took off her apron. "And, Tamiko, you can be in charge of crushing the cookies and candy for the mix-ins when it's slow. I'm going into the back to do some paperwork. Let me know if you need me!"

Sierra took her place in front of the register. I noticed that the crushed cookies were about to run out, so I went behind the counter, washed my hands, and got to work crushing up the cookies. There were several cookie-crushing methods, but Mrs. S.'s preferred method was to put the cookies into a plastic bag, seal it, and crush them with a rolling pin.

I got to work on a bag of chocolate cookies, watching them go from cookies to crushed crumbs. *Crushed, just like my dreams,* I thought.

Then the bell on the door tinkled, and a man walked up to the counter. I put down the rolling pin.

"How can I help you?" I asked.

"Hmm. I'm not sure," he replied. "I'm not sure what flavor to try. What do you recommend?"

"Vanilla," I replied. I didn't bother to try to convince him to order something more exciting. What was the point?

He raised his eyebrows but didn't argue. "Okay. One small vanilla sugar cone, please."

"Coming right up," I said with absolutely no joy in my voice. I made him the cone, handed it to him, and then went back to crushing cookies. The man paid Sierra, and the bell jingled as he left.

"You're not yourself today, Tamiko," Sierra said. "What about the Sprinkle Sundays sisters? Are we going to do a Sunday selfie later?"

"We could," I said, and I looked at Allie. "Unless you think it's a *Tamiko* idea."

Allie sighed. "Oh, Tamiko, I didn't mean it like that!" she said. She turned to Sierra. "Tamiko has an idea that we should make these Japanese cakes in the shop, and they look cool and everything, but I just don't see how it could work." She looked back at me. "But I didn't mean it in a bad way. You have good ideas, Tamiko. The unicorn sundae is a huge hit. Mom has been selling them all week."

"That wasn't even my idea," I pointed out. "It was MacKenzie's."

"Yes, but you're the one whose idea it was to sell them in the shop," Allie said. Then her face lit up, like she'd gotten an idea. "I know. Why don't we make a sundae and take a picture of it and put it on Super-Snap?"

"Are we allowed to do that?" I asked. "Isn't that wasting ice cream?"

"It's not wasting if we're using it for marketing," she said, brushing off my dig. "Besides, we can share it when we're done with the marketing, so it won't go to waste."

Marketing! I started feeling a little better. Allie was saying exactly the right things, and I knew she must have felt bad about—well, everything.

"Okay. Let's make an extra pretty one," I said. "Which means extra sprinkles."

The after-lunch crowd hadn't started yet, so we had time to make the perfect unicorn sundae. Two perfectly round, equal scoops of pink and blue ice cream. A luscious mountain of fluffy whipped cream. An artful scatter of mini-marshmallows and sprinkles—lots of sprinkles.

"Now, that looks too pretty to eat!" Sierra said.

"That is definitely going into our bellies," I promised. "But first, a photo."

I moved the sundae to one of the tables and got a few shots with my phone. Allie and Sierra did the same.

"It's too bad your mom doesn't have a SuperSnap account for the shop yet," I said.

"I'm working on her," Allie promised. "In the meantime we'll just have to count on hashtags."

"Hashtag unicorn?" Sierra suggested.

"That's good," I said. "But we also need something to let people know about the shop. So local people will find it."

"Hashtag Bayville Beach?" Allie asked.

"Brilliant!" I cried.

All three of us posted the photo with #Unicorn #IceCream #BayvilleBeach #UnicornSundae. I wanted the three of us to take a unicorn selfie, but then customers started pouring through the door.

"Sprinkle Sundays sisters, activate!" I said, and we hurried to our positions behind the counter.

"I'll put the sundae in the freezer, for later!" Allie promised.

Yes, I was still stinging from my crushing defeat. But I was glad to be having fun with my friends again—until Grumpy Guy came up to the counter.

I will never know his real name. I will forever refer to him as Grumpy Guy. And trust me, Grumpy Guy was not as adorable as those viral grumpy animals on social media. Not in any way, shape, or form.

Grumpy Guy walked up to the counter and stared at the menu.

"What's the difference between a small, a medium, and a large sundae?" he asked.

I picked up the three different cups and showed him.

"Which one is the small?" he asked.

"Uh, the smallest one," I said.

"Okay," he said. "I'll have a small butterscotch sundae with vanilla ice cream, walnuts, and a cherry on top."

"Would you like whipped cream on that?" I asked.

"Yes," he said.

"And what about sprinkles?" I asked.

He made a face. "No sprinkles. I hate sprinkles."

That was when I knew for sure that he had no soul. Who hated sprinkles?

I wrote down the order on my little green pad and passed it to Allie. Then I took the next order from a woman with two little kids. As I handed that order to Allie, she gave me the finished sundae. I checked it against the order I had written down. Vanilla ice cream, butterscotch sauce, walnuts, cherry, whipped cream. Perfect!

I handed it to Grumpy Guy. "Here you go, sir," I said.

"This has whipped cream," he said, passing it back to me. "I said no whipped cream."

"Um, you said yes to whipped cream," I said.

"I did not," he protested.

"You did. I wrote it down," I said. I showed him the order on the pad.

"Well, you wrote it down wrong," he said.

I looked at Allie.

"It's okay," she said. "I'll make another one."

It was a shame, because there was no way to take whipped cream off a sundae. It just didn't work like that. But I started to stress out. Would Allie be mad at me like when I'd dropped the sundae? I walked over to her.

"You heard him say he wanted whipped cream, right?" I whispered.

84

She nodded. "It's okay," she said. "My mom says she gets customers like this all the time. It's part of doing business." She squeezed my hand, which made me feel a little better.

Allie made another sundae, and I handed it to Grumpy Guy. He was impatiently tapping his fingers on the counter.

"How's this?" I asked.

"Is this a small?" he said. "It looks like a medium. Don't charge me for a medium."

"It is definitely a small," I said. "It just looks big because we are very generous with our ingredients here. Nothing but the best for our customers!"

I gave him the biggest, fakest smile I could manage.

Grumpy Guy humphed and then paid for his sundae. He didn't put a dime in the tip jar. And then he sat at a table *forever* using the shop's free Wi-Fi.

I understood that bad customers were the price of doing business. But the problem was, I was starting to think that maybe I didn't want to be in business anymore!

CHAPTER EIGHT

TUESDAY TROUBLES

My ponytail swung back and forth as I ran down the wooded path, being chased by twelve other girls.

They will never catch me! I told myself as I pressed on, running faster and faster.

No, I was not starring in a horror movie. It was Tuesday afternoon, and I was running a race as a member of the MLK cross-country team.

Do not get the wrong idea. I never used to love running. I didn't even like it very much. My favorite sport was softball—duh. But softball season didn't start until April, and if I were to sit around all fall, waiting for the season to start, I'd never be able to steal bases or run to catch pop-up balls.

Most athletes would just go to the gym. But like

I said earlier, I hated the gym showers. No one was going to drag me into one of those. My mom ran, so I had started going on runs with her. There were two problems with that. First, she talked when she ran, which was annoying. The second was that she ran insanely early in the morning. Sometimes we ran together on the weekends, but I'd decided to join the cross-country team, which ran at a more reasonable hour after school.

I heard shoes crunching on the path behind me. A girl with blond hair in braids passed me—Grace Riley. We'd never had anything in common until I'd joined the team. She nodded to me as she passed. I didn't mind so much because at least she was on the MLK team. I wasn't super-competitive, but I never liked it when girls from the opposing team passed me.

I picked up my pace a little bit, but I couldn't catch up to Grace. I heard more footsteps behind me and turned to see three girls, one from MLK and two from the Branchton Middle School team.

I pushed myself even faster. One of the Branchton girls passed me, but I kept the other two at bay.

Finally the finish line was in sight. I could see five

runners ahead of me, which would put me in sixth place. Not bad, out of seventeen girls.

I crossed the line and then bent over, hands on my knees.

"Yay, Tamiko!"

"You did it, Tamiko!"

I looked up to see my dad and Kai, cheering me on. I hadn't been expecting to see either of them there. Dad and Mom both worked at the college a few towns away, so they sometimes had off in the afternoon, depending on their class schedules. Kai's lone after-school activity was the business club. He'd never been into sports.

I walked up to them, sweating and panting.

"Hey," I said.

"Nice job, Tamiko," Dad said. "I'm very proud of you. You put a lot of effort into that final stretch."

"Yeah, well, sixth place," I said with a shrug.

"But MLK also got first, second, and fourth place," Kai added. "So I'm guessing that your team probably won."

"We can take you home, so you don't have to ride the bus," Dad said.

I nodded. "Great! Be right back!"

I ran off to check in with Coach Furman, looked at my recorded time, and then jogged back to Dad and Kai.

"Thanks for coming to see me," I said as we got into the car.

"I was also thinking that we could stop at Mrs. Shear's ice cream parlor on the way home," Dad said. "I haven't seen it yet."

"Sounds good to me," I said. "But before dinner?"

"Well, it's early still," Dad said. "And if you don't tell Mom, then I won't." He smiled at me in the rearview mirror. "Plus, Mom's making her casserole tonight." Now he grinned even bigger at me.

I'd suspected that Dad had an ulterior motive for coming to my meet, and for suggesting the ice cream parlor. Mom loved to make this casserole. Kai and I liked it—it was creamy and had mysterious but delicious ingredients in it. But Dad didn't really care for it. So he probably wanted to fill up on ice cream beforehand.

That didn't bother me at all, because after running two miles, I was pretty hungry. We drove into downtown Bayville and entered the shop.

It was four fifteen, and the shop was deserted,

except for Allie's mom, who was standing at the counter all by herself. She brightened up when we came in.

"Toshi, Tamiko, Kai!" she said. "Good to see you."

"Good to see you too," Dad said. "The place looks very nice."

"Very nice, and very slow," she said with a sigh.

"Is it always this slow?" Kai asked.

Mrs. S. shook her head. "No," she replied. "Tuesday is just the slowest day of the week, but I think that's because this is a beach town. Lots of people stay for three-day weekends, but they're all gone by Tuesday."

I looked up on the menu board and saw FLAVOR OF THE DAY: LAVENDER BLACKBERRY.

"Hey, you did a flavor of the day!" I said. "Is that the purple ice cream?"

She nodded. "Yes. I used blackberries, so it's naturally purple. It came out great."

I looked at Dad. "Can we order?" I asked, and he nodded. "Then I'll have a single scoop of Lavender Blackberry please, in a sugar cone."

As much as I thought that sugar cones were boring, I actually really liked them. When you wanted to really taste a flavor of ice cream, they were the best backdrop.

Mrs. S. handed me my cone. "Would you like a sprinkle of happy?" she asked.

I laughed. "Yes, please!"

Dad and Kai ordered their cones. Dad got the Banana Pudding, and Kai got the Kitchen Sink with chocolate sprinkles.

"Oh, man," Kai said after a few bites. "Mrs. Shear, this is awesome! This place should be packed every minute!"

"I told you," I said.

"It is delicious," my dad agreed.

We paid for our ice cream, said good-bye to Mrs. S., and headed home. We found Mom in the kitchen, busy working on her casserole.

"Hey, guys," she said. "How was the meet?"

"MLK won," I replied. "I placed sixth."

Mom wiped her hands and gave me a hug. "Good job!" she said.

"We stopped at Mrs. Shear's ice cream parlor," Kai said, and Mom glared at my dad but didn't say anything. "That ice cream is amazing. There is no reason why her shop should not be packed every day."

"She told you," I said. "It's a beach town. Nobody's around on Tuesdays."

"That's not true," Kai said. "Bayville has a year-round population of twenty-one thousand people. That's enough people to pack an ice cream shop on a Tuesday. She just has to up her marketing game."

"She totally does," I said. "She doesn't even have a page on social media."

Kai grinned. "I love a challenge," he said. "Want to help me?"

"Of course!" I answered.

"Tonight, after homework," he said mysteriously.

"Cool. I need to shower," I said. I went upstairs. Before I could shower, I got a text from Keiko.

Fun seeing you Saturday, T! Miss you!

I stared at the text. The whole thing with her and Ken liking each other had really gotten to me. It wasn't like I was jealous that they were closer, and it wasn't that I liked Ken too. I still thought boys were mainly gross and annoying.

I just liked how things used to be. Keiko, Ken, Tamiko. Or Allie, Sierra, Tamiko. I liked both groups exactly the way they were. And I did not want anything to upset the balance.

I texted back.

Miss you too! 😊

I wanted to talk to Keiko about the whole Ken thing, but now was not the time. I had a casserole to eat. And a plot to hatch with my brother, the business genius.

CHAPTER NINE
I'M MELTING . . .

As much as I hated admitting it, Kai was a very popular kid in his high school. As his sister, it was hard for me to be objective, but I thought there were a few reasons why he was popular. Some people would say Kai was handsome, and even though he said he didn't pay attention to fashion, he always managed to look pretty cool. He was outgoing and made friends easily. He had a lot of energy, and he used it to keep up on every trend out there. He knew the deets of every social media star, he would be the first one to send you a meme before it blew up, and he knew which songs were going to be popular before they even came out.

Kai was plugged in. So I knew that Kai was the perfect person to help Mrs. S. boost her business.

"You were right about my taiyaki proposal," I confessed to him Tuesday night as we sat down at his desk in his incredibly neat bedroom. "Mrs. S. said she'd think about it, but Allie kept bringing up all kinds of problems."

"I still think it's a good idea," Kai said. "But I think our first priority should be helping Mrs. Shear boost her Tuesday business. And I think that's a lot easier to do than making taiyaki, for now."

I nodded. "What were you thinking?" I asked him.

Kai started typing into his computer. "There are several marketing strategies geared specifically for food-service business," he said. "For example, Mrs. Shear could sell ice cream at a food festival like the one at the Japan center. It would raise more awareness about her business."

"Right, but it would have to be within traveling distance of Bayville," I said. "Because ice cream melts pretty fast. And that still doesn't solve the Tuesday problem, does it?"

"No, it doesn't," Kai agreed. "The most logical action to take would be to create some kind of Tuesday offer. A discount, or buy one, get one free. You said she doesn't have a social media presence?"

I shook my head. "Nope. Not yet."

Kai frowned. "That's too bad. E-mail is a great way to get out coupon offers. So are media sharing networks."

"Mrs. Shear is pretty old-school," I informed him.

"We can work with that," Kai said. He typed something into his computer, and an image of a supermarket coupon came up. "We'll go with a coupon. Everybody loves coupons!"

"Perfect!" I said. "Can I design it?"

"Sure," Kai said. "I'll help you with the wording. And we need to figure out what kind of discount would be best."

I yawned. "Awesome. Can we work on it during the week? I'm beat."

"No prob," Kai said.

I left, thinking how lucky I was to have a big brother who didn't tease me or bully me like the big brothers in some TV shows. Kai was pretty cool.

The problem was, Kai was busy, and so was I. I had a big science test coming up on Friday, so between cross-country and studying, I had no time to work on the coupon. And Kai was busy with the internship he'd gotten himself in the advertising office of the local TV station, WKSC.

I was hoping to get the coupon ready with Kai on Saturday, after my meet, but he was at a WKSC event all day, and then he went out with his friends at night. Luckily, he always woke up early, so I cornered him Sunday morning.

It took longer than I'd thought to get the coupons ready. We decided to make one hundred, to start. We figured out the exact wording, and I designed them on my laptop. Then Mom took us to the office supply store to make the copies.

Back home I had to cut out all the coupons by hand. I had been unprepared for my taiyaki proposal, but I wanted to really impress Mrs. S. with this plan. I wanted to make sure that the Tuesday coupons would not be something that people would just throw away, or stick into their purses and forget about. These coupons needed to be memorable, and to do that I needed glitter.

I was in my DIY room with the music blasting, and glitter all over my hands, when Mom barged in, scaring me.

"Tamiko!" she said. "It's almost one o'clock! Don't you have to be at the ice cream shop?"

"Oh, gosh!" I said, looking up. "I just have a few more to finish. I'll be ready in five."

"Don't you think we should leave now?" Mom asked. "You'll already be a half hour late."

"I know I should probably leave now," I said, "but then I won't be able to show Mrs. S. these coupons until next Sunday!"

Mom gave me the look that said, *I'll let you face the consequences*, then left me alone. It was actually ten more minutes before I finished, and I had to wash the glitter off my hands and put on my work T-shirt.

By the time I got into the store, the clock on the wall read 1:35. There was a line of customers at the counter, and Mrs. S. was taking orders.

"There you are, Tamiko!" she said. "We were wondering where you were."

"I was working on these!" I said, waving the coupons. "Kai gave me this great idea, and he helped me make them."

I walked behind the counter as Mrs. S. was passing a milkshake to the customer in front of her. I held a coupon up to show her.

"Remember Tuesday, when we came in and you talked about how it's always so slow?" I asked. "Well, my brother and I came up with these coupons."

Tuesday Treat!
Share a Sprinkle of Happy!
Buy One, Get Half Off a Second!

Offer is good for all cups, cones, sundaes, shakes, sodas, and mix-ins. One coupon per customer. This coupon is valid any Tuesday from noon to 5 p.m.

To finish them off I had used a glitter pen to add sparkles that looked like sprinkles on each one.

"What do you think?" I asked. "They're incentive for people to come in on Tuesdays. And they are too beautiful to throw out! People will keep them and remember to use them. Kai said if this works well, we should think up promotions for other days of the week too."

While I'd been talking, more people had come into the shop. The woman closest to the counter eyed the coupon in my hand.

"Buy one, get one half off?" she asked. "I'd come in on Tuesday for that. Can I have one?"

I couldn't have planned that moment better myself. It was perfect! I looked at Mrs. S. She read the type carefully, and I waited for what seemed like an hour but was only a few seconds.

"Sure," she said, handing the woman a coupon.

"I'd like one!" said another woman behind her.

"Tell you what, Tamiko," Mrs. S. said. "Let's keep them by the register and have Sierra give them out. We don't want to get glitter in the ice cream."

"Good thinking," I said.

"All right. I'm going into the back, girls," Mrs. S. said. "Tamiko, please jump right in so that people aren't waiting too long."

"You got it, Mrs. S.!" I said cheerfully. Mrs. S. took a coupon with her to the office.

I was feeling pretty good. Mrs. S. hadn't exactly praised the coupons, but she hadn't rejected them either. Over the next half hour I made thirteen cones and five cups, and Allie put together five sundaes, two milkshakes, and four mix-ins. Business was booming!

Oh, and one of the customers was a woman in pink scrubs whom I remembered right away. It was the nurse! She had brought two other nurses with her.

"Three unicorn sundaes?" I asked when I saw her, and she laughed.

"You really brightened my day the last time I was here," she said. "That unicorn sundae was delicious, but today I was thinking of something more choco-late."

"Kitchen Sink hot fudge sundae?" I suggested.

"I completely trust you," she said. "Bring it on!"

"I'll try a unicorn sundae, though," said one of her nurse friends. The other nurse ordered a cup of vanilla, but I didn't give her a hard time about it. I caught myself humming a tune as I scooped out the vanilla ice cream. It was funny how a nice customer could make you feel happy just as much as a rude customer could ruin your mood.

Since I'd come in late, I hadn't had time to check in with Sierra or Allie. We hadn't taken our Sunday selfie. They were both being pretty quiet, but I figured it was because we were busy.

When it finally slowed down, I wiped my hands on a towel and picked up my phone. "Is it too late for our Sunday selfie?" I asked.

"I don't know," Allie said. "Is it too *late*?" She emphasized the last word. Before I could ask what she meant by that, three kids came into the shop.

I recognized them as friends from Allie's new school. The boy, Colin, had a cute smile. I couldn't remember the two girls' names, but I was pretty sure these were the nice girls that Allie had met, not the mean girls that she called the Mean Team.

"Colin! Amanda! Eloise!" Allie cried, and she ran around the counter to hug them.

"We saw your SuperSnap, so we came by," Colin said.

"What SuperSnap?" I asked.

Colin walked over to me and held out his phone. The picture was a selfie of Allie and Sierra, each holding up an ice cream cone. Their mouths were open, like they were screaming.

We all scream for ice cream! #IceCream #SundayGoals #BayvilleBeach

"That's cute," I said, but I was feeling a little bit hurt. "It's just missing something. Me!"

Allie ignored me. "What do you guys want?" she asked her new friends.

"I was thinking of trying a unicorn sundae," said Amanda.

"I need a Chocolate Mint Chip shake, please," said Eloise.

"I'll have a Butterscotch Chocolate Chunk cone," Colin said.

Allie gave him the biggest smile.

"I've got the butterscotch," I said. "Will that be a regular cone, Colin, or do you want something fancy?"

"Regular cone is fine," he said. "Tamiko, right?"

"That's me!" I said. I wondered if Allie talked about us to her new friends.

The shop got busy again for a while, but Allie's friends hung around until things got quiet again, and then Allie went over and talked to them for a few minutes. Finally they left.

Sierra looked at Allie. "Colin is really nice," she said, and she wiggled her eyebrows.

Allie blushed. "Yes, he is nice. That's why he's my friend."

"He's kind of cute, too," Sierra said.

"Sierra!" Allie squealed.

"Why is it that every time a boy and a girl are friends, people assume they like each other in a romantic way?" I asked, thinking of Keiko and Ken. "Can't boys and girls be friends?"

"Of course they can," Allie said. "Just like me and Colin."

Sierra rolled her eyes. "Of course that's possible. I'm just saying . . . Allie, he was following your Super-Snap. And then he came to see you."

103

"He came to get ice cream," Allie corrected her.

"It was a good SuperSnap," I said. "Although, I wish you guys had waited for me. You know—Sprinkle Sundays?"

"Tamiko, you were so late!" Allie said. "And I texted you, but you didn't answer. As far as we knew, you were bailing."

"I would never bail!" I protested. "I was *working*. Working on the coupons."

"But you were supposed to be working *here*," Allie pointed out.

I looked to Sierra, hoping to get some backup. She shrugged. "We didn't know what was happening, Tamiko," she said. "We were worried, but it was also a little unfair because we were trying to do the work of three people."

I was starting to feel very un-fabulous. This was my third official Sprinkle Sunday, and for the third time, something was stepping all over my happy. First Allie had freaked about the dropped sundae. Then she and Mrs. S. had crushed my brilliant taiyaki idea. And now Allie was giving me a hard time for being late, and Sierra wasn't backing me up. And Mrs. S. hadn't said anything—

But just as I was thinking this, Mrs. S. suddenly appeared at my side.

"Sierra, you can cash out the register now," she said. "And, Tamiko, can I talk to you in the back for a moment?"

"Sure," I said, and I had a feeling that my day was going to get even more un-fabulous.

I went into the back room. Mrs. S. sat on the edge of her desk.

"Tamiko, I appreciate all the hard work you put into the coupons," she said. "But I have a problem with you being late today."

I nodded. "I'm sorry. I was finishing up the coupons."

"And they're great," she said. "But I gave Sierra a warning when she was late, and I'm going to give you one too. You can't be late for your shift. If you're going to work here, I need a commitment from you that you can be on time."

I felt like a slowly melting pool of ice cream.

"I will be," I promised. My voice sounded small and weird.

"Good," she said. "And please don't get me wrong—I do need help with marketing. But maybe we can figure out a way for you to help me with that some other time, not during your shift. I can pay you separately for that."

That made me feel a teensy bit better. "So, you like the coupons?"

"I think they're a great idea," she said. "I'm not sure if giving half off the second order will be profitable or not, but we'll test them out. Since the customers had already seen them, I didn't want to take them away."

That had been my fault too, I guessed, from the way she said it.

Mrs. S. said, "Next time you have an idea, let me know, and we'll discuss it when it's good for both of us, before you do a lot of work and before we introduce it to the customers."

"Sure," I said in my tiny voice. But I was steaming inside. Mrs. S. did not seem to appreciate all the hard work I'd put into those coupons—the coupons that the customers had gone absolutely nuts for!

"Are you okay, Tamiko?" Mrs. S. asked.

"Yes, I'm fine," I lied.

"Great," Mrs. S. said. "Let's get you paid. I'll see you next week!"

I walked out to the front. Allie was counting the tips.

"Great day!" she said. "We made almost twenty-five dollars each just in tips!"

"I shouldn't get as much as you two," I said, still in my flat, melted-ice-cream voice. "You know, for being late."

Allie and Sierra looked at each other.

"Nah, don't worry about it," Allie said. "It's fine."

Mrs. S. gave us our shift pay, and Sierra started talking about this fabulous dress she had seen at the mall that she was saving up for. Allie had a million questions about it, but I didn't chime in. I put my money in my bag, said "See ya!" and then walked outside to wait for my mom to pick me up.

A minute later Sierra came outside.

"Tamiko, what's wrong?" she asked. "Did Mrs. S. get on your case about being late? Don't worry about it. She did that to me too."

"I'm fine," I repeated.

"You don't sound fine," Sierra said. "Not fine at all. If anything, you sound the opposite of fine."

"Fine," I said in a singsong voice, and then, to my relief, Mom pulled up. "See you tomorrow." I waved to Sierra, and she just looked at me with her big, brown, puppy-dog eyes.

I climbed into the passenger seat.

"Hello, Tamiko," Mom said. "Did you get your sprinkle of happy today?"

I didn't answer. I didn't know what to say. The promise I'd made to her came back to haunt me.

When it stops being fun, I'll quit.

CHAPTER TEN
☺ AND ☹

Mom, thankfully, didn't press me for an answer. When we got home, I took off my dirty clothes without being asked, showered, and changed into leggings and an oversize T-shirt. When I was done, my phone dinged.

Please tell me what's wrong! Sierra texted. **I'm worried about you!**

I sighed and looked at my phone screen. I didn't know what to say to Sierra. I honestly felt like quitting our Sprinkle Sundays crew, but I didn't know how to tell her. I knew she'd try to talk me out of it. Plus, I wasn't even sure if I wanted to quit. I was so confused!

The door to my room was open, and Kai poked his head in.

"How did Mrs. Shear like the coupons?" he asked.

I sighed. "She liked them. I guess. She was mad that I was late, and she said we should have discussed them with her first."

Kai nodded. "Well, you shouldn't have been late. You should arrive early to your job if you want to make a good impression. Plus she's right about showing them to her first. She should approve any kind of promotion. I mean, we thought it made sense, but she knows about her profits and what she can afford to offer. I should have told you that."

I flopped down onto my bed. "Well, thanks for telling me now!" I said, scowling. Then I sat up. "Kai, what do you do when you have a decision to make?"

"A list of pros and cons," he replied without hesitating. "I write them down, and then I compare them. The answer is usually pretty clear."

"Thanks!" I said, and as Kai walked away, I jumped up and went into my DIY room and found a piece of graph paper. I drew a line down the middle.

I drew ☺ on the left and ☹ on the right.

Working at the ice cream shop had seemed like a great idea at first. The shop was super-cool, and I liked the idea of earning money, and then there was the whole thing of not getting to see Allie at school anymore. But so far I had been mostly miserable there. I didn't want to quit, but I didn't really want to keep working there either.

In the ☺ column I wrote:

> Being with Allie and Sierra
> Extra money
> I love ice cream

In the ☹ column I wrote:

> Allie gets too uptight in the shop
> My ideas aren't appreciated
> Mrs. S. lectures = not fun

I stared at the two columns. They were even. How was I supposed to make a decision?

I went to Kai's room and knocked on his door.

"What is it?" he replied.

I pushed open the door. "What do you do if the two columns are even?" I asked.

"Well," he said, "you made your pros and cons awfully fast. Put some more thought into it, and I'm sure you'll come up with some more pros or cons. Or consider if one of your pros or cons has more weight than the others."

"What do you mean?" I asked.

"Well. For example, one pro of eating a bag of extra-hot taco chips might be that they taste good," he said, "but one con is that your guts will burn for the next twelve hours. So even though there is one pro and one con, the burning-guts factor carries more weight. Or at least it does for me. I learned that the hard way."

"Got it," I said, and I went back to my DIY room. I studied the list, and then I added one more in the ☺ column:

Nice customers

But then I added four more to the ☹ column:

Mean customers
Cleaning up hot-fudge spills
Getting orders wrong
No taiyaki

The answer was clear. There were more cons than pros. Just then Sierra texted me again.

Tamiko, u there? ☺

I texted her back. I have to quit Sprinkle Sundays. It's making me 😣.

Nooooooooooooooo! 😵

Then I heard my dad's voice. "Tamiko! Kai! Please come down for dinner!"

I left my phone in my room so that I wouldn't get yelled at for using it at the dinner table. Dad had cooked dinner for us: tofu, rice, miso soup, and pickled vegetables.

We were just finishing dinner when I realized the time.

"Grandpa's up!" I cried, and jumped up from the table.

Mom looked at Dad. "I thought you were going to talk to him about not interrupting dinner. If he just waited fifteen minutes . . ."

"It's his routine," Dad said. "He likes to call as soon as he wakes up."

Grandpa Sato and I exchanged greetings.

"Are you watching a game?" he asked.

"It's a night game tonight," I informed him. "I'm going to watch it if Mom and Dad let me."

"We need to do a homework check first," Mom chimed in.

"What about you?" I asked. "Is your team playing?"

"They played last night," he said. "They won. Ryota Tanaka hit a three-run homer."

I searched my mind for the name. "The rookie?" I asked.

Grandpa nodded. "Yes. He is a very interesting fellow," he said. "Did you know that he wanted to quit the game in college? But his coach gave him an inspiring speech, and he stuck with the sport. He is no quitter, that Tanaka."

"Nope," I said, and I was wondering if Grandpa Sato had some weird grandpa mojo that let him know that I had just unofficially quit my job at the ice cream shop.

"Tamiko, come finish your dinner and let Kai talk to Grandpa," Mom said.

"Sure," I said. *"Sayonara, Ojiichan!"*

"*Sayonara*, Tamiko-chan!" he said, and he waved at me.

After dinner I went back up to my room and stared at my list. Clearly there were more cons than pros. I snapped a picture of the list to show Sierra the next day at school. Once she saw it, I knew she'd understand.

"I'm sorry, Grandpa," I said, alone in my room. "I am no Tanaka."

CHAPTER ELEVEN

COLD TOTS, WARM HEART

"Excellent work, Tamiko," Mr. Rivera said. "Nice, clean lines."

"Thanks," I said.

It was Monday morning, and in art class we were still working on perspective. The week before, Mr. Rivera had instructed us to take a photo of a room with furniture in it, and I'd chosen the ice cream parlor, of course. Then we'd used the photo as a guide for creating drawings with a 3-D effect.

"Where is your vanishing point?" he asked.

"Right here," I said, and I put my finger on the spot where the counter met the adjoining wall.

"Very good," he said. "Keep going."

I stared at the vanishing point in my drawing of

the empty ice cream parlor. Soon I would be vanishing from the ice cream parlor. Just as soon as I told Allie's mom that I was quitting.

I started adding details to the drawing. The hanging cone-shaped lights. The menu board. Then I added a stick-figure Allie behind the counter. And a stick-figure Sierra behind the register, with lots of wild hair. I drew a stick figure with a mustache and a frown sitting at one of the tables—Grumpy Guy.

I didn't add myself to the picture. I stared at it. Who would take the orders? Who would encourage customers to move beyond their prisons of vanilla, chocolate, and strawberry? Not me.

The bell rang, and I headed to English class. I kept waiting for MacKenzie to slide into the chair next to me, but she never showed up.

That's weird, I thought. *I saw her in homeroom.*

And then it hit me—maybe MacKenzie'd had her testing and had been moved to a different class. I couldn't wait to ask her at lunchtime.

But when I got to the cafeteria, Sierra marched up to me as soon as I got in the lunch line.

"We need to talk!" she said. "You are not going to quit!"

"Okay, okay," I said. "I have something to show you. But wait till I get my food. It's Tots today."

Say what you want about cafeteria food, but it is impossible to hate Tater Tots. I got my lunch and brought it back to the table, but Sierra didn't give me a chance to eat one bite before she launched into me.

"You can't quit!" she said. "We can work it out, Tamiko. Me, you, and Allie need our Sprinkle Sundays! Without them, things just won't be the same."

"But I have a list," I said, and I scrolled through my phone to show her. "A list of pros and cons. And see? The cons outweigh the pros."

Sierra studied the list. "No, they don't," she said.

"Of course they do," I corrected her. "There are more cons than pros."

"Yes, but the cons don't *outweigh* the pros," she said. She took out her phone and started sending me photos. My phone kept beeping, and photos of me, Sierra, and Allie kept popping up. At the beach. In the bookstore. In Allie's kitchen. At the mall. In the ice cream shop.

"Okay, I get it!" I said.

"Do you?" Sierra asked. "Because the first thing

on your pros list is 'being with Allie and Sierra.' And that should count for, like, a million! Way more than cleaning up hot fudge. Wiping up hot fudge takes, what? Five minutes. But think of all the years we've got invested in our friendship. You can't just throw that away."

It was exactly as Kai had said, about one of the pros or cons carrying more weight. So me, Allie, and Sierra were like Kai's burning guts. Well, not exactly, but you know what I mean. Maybe I hadn't thought this through. Because when I tried to imagine my life without Allie and Sierra in it, I just couldn't. I mean, I *could* live without them. They weren't like food and water; it's not like I would die without them. But life definitely wouldn't be as much fun.

"Fine," I said. "I won't quit."

Sierra hugged me. "Yay! I knew I could convince you!"

"But hear me out," I said. "I mean, working at the shop doesn't have to be the only time when we see Allie, does it? Because I think it's better if she's not always our boss. I need to see the relaxed, fun Allie sometimes."

"That makes sense," Sierra said. She started texting. In a few seconds she got a text back.

"We're going to the movies on Saturday," she said. "In the afternoon. That's plenty of time after your track meet, right?"

"It's cross-country," I corrected her. "But yes."

MacKenzie came running up with her lunch bag.

"Where were you?" I asked.

"I got moved to a different English class," she said. "And then I stayed after to talk to the teacher about some stuff."

"So is it a good thing?" I asked.

MacKenzie smiled. "Definitely a good thing."

I held up my phone. "Lunch squad selfie!"

MacKenzie and Sierra squeezed in next to me. Sierra smiled, I made my perfect selfie face, and MacKenzie stuck out her tongue. It was a great picture. I posted it on SuperSnap with the caption: Lunch squad goals: Eat your Tots before they get cold!

"Sorry, Tamiko. I forgot about your Tots," Sierra said. "But I'm glad we talked."

"Me too," I said, and I picked one up and took a bite. My Tots might have been cold, but I was feeling pretty warm and fuzzy inside.

"That was the worst movie ever!" I complained as Sierra, Allie, and I walked out of Bayville Cinemas.

"It was not!" Sierra said, but she was laughing.

"Okay, Miss Drama Club, you don't think the acting was terrible?" I asked. "Like when the guy was fake crying? 'Noooo! Dr. Nebula! Don't die!'"

I did my best impression of the guy in the movie, and Sierra and Allie started cracking up. But Sierra still defended the movie.

"Crying isn't easy to do on cue," she said.

I turned to Allie. "And what about you, Miss Books? Did you think that plot made any sense at all?"

She shook her head. "You're right. That plot had more holes than a piece of Swiss cheese."

I nodded triumphantly. "Case closed."

We strolled down the street. There was a big multiplex in the mall, but Bayville still had a tiny theater in the middle of town that catered to the beach crowd, mostly showing kids' movies and superhero movies, which was what we had just seen.

"What do you want to do now?" Allie asked.

"I don't know," Sierra said. "I'm kind of hungry."

"We should get something to eat," I suggested.

We glanced down the street at all of the shops. Harry's Falafel, the Dunes Deli, Molly's . . . Then we looked at one another, all thinking the same thing.

"Ice cream!"

CHAPTER TWELVE
SPRINKLE SISTERS FOR LIFE!

I took Kai's advice and showed up twenty minutes early to my shift the next day. I told myself that I wasn't going to worry about coupons, or marketing, or coming up with new ideas. I was going to take orders and make ice cream cones. And I was going to do it better than anyone else in the history of ice cream shops.

Mrs. S. was wiping down the counter when I came in.

"I'm glad you're early, Tamiko," she said. "Can I talk to you in the back?"

Oh no, I thought. For a second I was convinced that Mrs. S. was going to fire me! After I had already decided not to quit! But I glanced over at Allie, who was crushing candy behind the mix-ins, and her blue eyes were twinkling happily. Allie wouldn't look happy if I were about to get fired. I was pretty sure of that.

"Sure," I said, and I followed Mrs. S. to her desk. She sat down and flipped open her laptop.

"I have a few things to show you," she said. "First, this."

A site popped up, and there it was—a page for the shop!

"No way! You did it!" I cheered.

"Allie helped me set it up," she explained. "And I already started inviting people to like it."

"That is awesome," I said.

"I have set it up so that you can post photos to the page, Tamiko," she went on. "I'd like that to be part of your job. How does that sound?"

"That sounds great!" I said.

Mrs. S. smiled. "Perfect," she said. Then she flipped open a folder on her desk to reveal a stack of professionally printed Tuesday Treat coupons! They weren't covered in glitter, but there was sprinkle art all over the coupon. I got that warm fuzzy feeling inside again. So Mrs. S. had liked my ideas after all! To think that I had almost quit this great job. I actually shuddered a little, thinking how close I had come to leaving, and what a mistake that would have been.

"The coupons were a terrific idea," she said. "They have definitely increased my Tuesday business. So if you have any other ideas, I'd love to hear them. But before or after your shift."

I nodded. "Got it!"

"I want you to know how much I appreciate you, Tamiko," Mrs. S. said. "It is so sweet that you want to help the business succeed."

"This business deserves to succeed," I said. "And besides, the marketing stuff is fun."

Mrs. S. stood up. "Awesome. Now, Allie is crushing the mix-ins, so feel free to take some photos until it gets busy."

I took a few steps, and then I turned back to Mrs. S. "So, would you say that I'm sort of your unofficial social media director?"

"Sure," Mrs. S. replied. "You could say that."

I walked back into the parlor, grinning like crazy. A few minutes before, I had been sure I was going to get fired. But now I was the unofficial social media director of the trendiest ice cream shop on the coast!

Do I have a business card program on my laptop? I wondered.

Sierra came in, exactly on time, as I was snapping photos of Allie crushing the mix-ins.

"Hola, chicas!" she said. "What's happening?"

"Tamiko is uploading some photos onto Molly's new website page!" Allie reported. "And Sierra, the napkins need to be refilled, if you don't mind, *chica*."

"Why would I mind?" Sierra asked.

"Wow, you are extra cheerful today," I said.

She smiled. "I'm just happy that the Sprinkle Sundays team is still together."

Allie looked confused. We had never told her that I had almost quit.

Thankfully, a bunch of customers came in at that moment, and I recognized them. It was the dad with the cute little girls who had ordered unicorn sundaes a few weeks before.

"How can I help you?" I asked. "Three unicorn sundaes?"

The girls nodded shyly. I wrote up the order and gave it to Allie.

"Three unicorn sundaes coming right up!" I said. Then Grumpy Guy came in and gazed at the menu with his beady eyes. I steeled myself. I was not going to let him get to me this time.

"Hi! Can I help you?" I asked.

"I feel like having a sundae, but I don't know what to get," he said.

"How about a unicorn sundae?" I suggested. Allie had just handed me one, and I held it up to show him.

He grimaced. "Unicorns are stupid. Dragons are way cooler."

"Right!" I said, keeping my voice cheerful. "One moment, sir."

I handed the three unicorn sundaes to the dad and then turned back to Grumpy Guy. "How about a dragon sundae, then?"

He looked interested. "What's a dragon sundae?"

I thought quickly, going over in my head what topping ingredients the shop had. "It's . . . it's Chocolate Mint Chip ice cream with fiery cinnamon candies and chocolate spikes."

"That sounds good," he said.

I held up our three serving cups. "Would you like small, medium, or large?"

"Small, please," he replied.

I wrote down the order on my little green pad.

Then I showed it to Grumpy Guy.

"Is this correct?" I asked him.

He picked it up and scrutinized it, squinting. "Yes," he said. "You have very neat handwriting."

"Thank you," I said. I handed the order to Allie. "One dragon sundae, please."

Allie had been watching the whole exchange, so she knew what to do. She scooped some green Chocolate Mint Chip ice cream into a cup. She sprinkled on some red cinnamon candies. Then she took a square of the chocolate that we used for the mix-ins, cut it into rough chunks, and stuck them into the ice cream, like dragon spikes. I saw her reach for the sprinkles and stopped her.

"No!" I hissed. "He hates sprinkles!"

Allie nodded and handed me the sundae.

"Here you go, sir," I said to Grumpy Guy. "One small dragon sundae."

He studied it carefully. Then he brought it to Sierra and paid for it. She gave him his change.

Clink! I stared in amazement as coins fell into our tip jar.

I couldn't believe it! Grumpy Guy had given us a tip! Probably a very small tip, but still!

More customers came in after that, and I couldn't say that the dragon sundae took off the way the unicorn sundae had. But when Grumpy Guy left, I turned to Allie and high-fived her.

"Victory over Grumpy Guy!" I cheered.

"Who? Oh, him?" she said, and then she started cracking up.

"He actually tipped us this time," Sierra said.

"I know! I saw!" I told her.

We quieted down when a new customer came in.

"Hi," the customer said. "A friend told me about your ice cream shop, and she said you have the best ice cream around."

"We do," I assured her.

"Hmm," she said. "I'd love to try your Cereal Milk ice cream. That sounds delicious."

Allie chimed in. "It is," she said. "Mom got the idea after seeing me and my little brother drinking the milk left over from our cereal."

"I'll take a small cup, please," the woman said. "No, wait, a waffle cone!"

"You got it," I said, and then I started to scoop the ice cream into her cone.

"I just love ice cream," the woman went on. "You

know, I was just in Manhattan, and I had the most amazing thing. Have you ever had taiyaki?"

I couldn't believe my ears. "Yes," I said. "I've had traditional taiyaki, and also taiyaki with ice cream."

"That's what I had in Manhattan!" she cried. "It was so good! How genius is that, to top taiyaki with ice cream?"

I nodded enthusiastically. "I know, right! I had some at a festival two weeks ago. It was amazing."

She frowned. "Oh, you got it at a festival. I was hoping someplace around here was selling it."

"Not yet," I replied, and handed the cone to her. "Please pay at the register," I said.

When the woman left, I turned to Allie. "Maybe we shouldn't give up on the taiyaki idea," I said. "We could do it one day a week. Taiyaki Tuesdays. Or even Taiyaki Sundays, and I could work the machine."

"That might work," Allie admitted.

I wanted to run into the back and talk to Mrs. S., but I remembered my promise to her. Then I promised myself that I would come up with a proposal—a real one this time, with Kai's help. I was not giving up on the taiyaki!

Four more customers came in—and I knew them.

They were all in eighth grade at MLK. Ewan Kim, Jake DeStefano, Connor Jackson, and Sean Hunter. Sierra shot me a look when they came in, and her eyes widened. They were some of the most popular boys at MLK, and I already knew that Sierra thought that Jake was "seriously cute."

Ewan spoke first. "Hey, um, you're Tamiko, right? From art class?" he asked.

"Um, yeah," I said, and I felt myself blush. Why was I blushing?

"Okay, so can I please get a vanilla cone? With rainbow sprinkles?" he asked.

"Sure," I said, and I made it for him. I put the sprinkles on, and then I said, automatically, "Here's your sprinkle of happy!"

Jake and Connor started to laugh obnoxiously loudly. My face was burning. Why had I said that in front of these boys? Whhhyyyy?

But Ewan was smiling at me. "Thanks," he said.

I nodded to Sierra. "You pay there."

The other boys were still laughing when I took their orders. Connor and Sean wanted milkshakes, and Jake asked for *extra* sprinkles on his cone. When I handed it to him, I made sure not to say the sprinkles line.

"Aw, come on. Where's my sprinkle of happy?" he asked. "I asked for *extra* sprinkles. I thought I'd get an *extra-big* sprinkle of happy!"

I ignored him and turned to help the customers who had just walked in. Then I heard a commotion over by the register and turned my head to see what was going on.

Connor had grabbed the tub of rainbow sprinkles from behind the counter. He stuck his hand into it and threw some at Jake!

"Here's your sprinkle of happy!" Connor said.

"Guys, no!" Sierra cried.

They ignored her. Jake dipped his hand into the tub and tossed some sprinkles at Connor.

I marched away from my customers. "Hey, cut that out! That is not cool!"

But the boys were out of control. Ewan and Sean grabbed sprinkles too, and they were all throwing them at one another! Then Connor dumped the whole tub of sprinkles onto Jake's head!

I'd had it.

"Stop that right now!" I yelled, and the boys did stop, stunned at how loud I was. "Do you know how much those sprinkles cost?" I asked.

Sierra joined in. "You think you're funny, but every penny counts at a small business!" she shouted. "Not to mention that now we have to stop serving our customers so that we can clean up your big mess! You're being rude to our other customers."

The customers waiting in line applauded Sierra for that. Jake, Connor, and Sean all ran out, like jerks. Ewan started to follow them, but then he stopped.

"I can help you clean up," he said. He didn't look any of us in the eyes.

"Great," I said. "I'll get the broom and dustpan."

"I'll refill the sprinkles," Allie said.

I quickly returned with the broom and dustpan, and Ewan got to work sweeping the sprinkles off the floor. Sierra wiped down the countertops. I got back to taking orders and delivered them to Allie when she came back in with more sprinkles.

"Mom says thank you," she said. "It wasn't your fault."

"No, it was those jerks," I said, and then I realized that Ewan was still there. He had finished sweeping up the sprinkles, and then he left without a word. But then Sierra noticed something.

"There's ten bucks next to the register," she said. "I think Ewan left it."

"Well, maybe he's not such a jerk," I muttered. "But the other three are."

The rest of the customers told us we'd done a good job handling things, and they all asked for a sprinkle of happy, probably just to make us feel better.

Then the last customers left, and Allie walked over to Sierra and then to me and gave us each a hug.

"What was that for?" I asked.

"For being such good friends, and for standing up for the shop," she said. "I'm sorry I was being so uptight about the shop, but I want you to know that it means a lot that you care about Molly's too. I am so lucky to have my BFFs working with me!"

"And we're lucky to be working here," I said. "Sprinkle Sundays selfie!"

Allie, Sierra, and I got together, and I took the picture. Then I posted it on SuperSnap with a caption.

Sprinkle Sundays sisters!

And of course I tagged #Mollys #Bayville #BestIceCreamEver.

I posted it to the page and smiled when I looked at the shot. The three of us together seemed just right—the perfect Sunday combination.

Sprinkle SUNDAYS

DON'T MISS BOOK 3:
THE PURR-FECT SCOOP

I knew it had to be here somewhere! I just had to find it. I tied my long, brown hair into a ponytail to get it out of my way, and then I began searching slowly but surely, room by room, throughout the house.

My first stop was our clean but messy bright yellow kitchen, where I circled the cluttered table, sifted carefully through the pile of newspapers and magazines for recycling, roamed around the packed countertops (small appliances, jars and bins, piles of mail) and the jumbly kitchen island and even into the little closet with the washer and dryer, but no luck. My *abuela*— my mom's mom—is from Cuba and is super-religious; she always tells us to say a prayer to Saint Anthony when we lose something.

I felt a little silly asking a dead saint for help finding a comic book, but I was desperate. I'd borrowed it from my friend Cecelia, and I had to give it back to her at our Comic Book Club meeting after school on Monday. That only gave me two days to find it.

My *abuela* says the key to finding things, besides saying the little prayer, is that you have to *really* look, even in places you think you've already checked or places where you couldn't even imagine the thing being.

I went all through the living/dining room area, lifting sofa cushions, flipping through all the colorful needlepoint throw pillows my dad had made, peeking behind the bright watercolors of birds that my mom did for fun, looking underneath the box lid of the half-done jigsaw puzzle on the dining room table— nothing! I wandered into my parents' home office, but it was so immaculate, I could see at a glance that it wasn't on either of their back-to-back desktops or the low chest that held copies of their research, their patients' files, and more. The only place my parents were neat was in their offices, both here and at work. I couldn't really criticize them for messiness, though; I was messy and disorganized too. I think we all always thought we'd get back to a project, or find some time to clean up later, or organize our things, and then we would get busy and never did.

Upstairs, I went into their bedroom, where their bed was still unmade and clothing was strewn on chair-backs and across the small love seat by the window. A large oil painting of Cuban storefronts, painted by my dad's dad, hung proudly above my mom's dresser. She loved that picture but my dad didn't. Their families both emigrated to America when they were babies, in 1973, and while my mom was dying to go back for a visit, my dad said he never would. He didn't even like to talk about Cuba.

I sighed. Nothing in their room, nothing in their bathroom—thank goodness, because all their towels were damp and heaped in a pile; if the comic were there, it would surely have been ruined. I knew it wasn't in my room, because that's what had started this whole search. That only left one more possibility: my twin sister Isabel's room.

Unfortunately, that room was currently off-limits to me.

Isa's door was closed tightly, something she'd taken to doing since school had started this year. I wouldn't have been surprised if it was locked, even. She'd left earlier this afternoon, but I wasn't sure when she was due to return, and I dared not enter without her permission or I'd face her wrath.

I stood on the landing outside her door, my arms folded, my foot tapping in place as I thought. Finally I decided: Saint Anthony would want me to look. I was sure of it!

I put my hand on her doorknob.

Did I dare open the door?

Slowly, slowly, I turned the handle, my senses aflame for any sign of her return. The door was not locked, it turned out, and the handle turned easily.

The door began to open, and my eyes strained for a glimpse of a room I hadn't seen inside in more than six weeks. And then . . . *BANG!* The back door slammed downstairs!

I pulled Isabel's door closed, released the handle, and scurried back to my room, where I flung myself onto my bed, trying to look natural.

"Hello?" I called. I assumed it was Isa because my parents had returned to their clinic after our big Saturday lunch as usual.

There was no reply, only the sound of firm footsteps stomping across the floor below and then heading up the stairs.

"Isa?" I called.

Suddenly she was at my door. "Were you just in my room?" she demanded.

"What? Me? No! Seriously? Jeez!" *How on earth did she know?*

Isabel was carrying a big brown box. It had holes cut all round it, and something inside it was making noise.

"What's in the box?" I asked.

She hesitated and then turned on her heel and went to her room without answering me.

I waited a second, and then, intrigued, I stood to follow her. She opened her door, flipped on the lights with her elbow, and crossed the room to her desk. I was right behind her, and it surprised me that she didn't slam the door in my face as she usually would have. I stayed in the doorway anyway, just to be safe.

Isabel and I are technically identical twins, but no one mixes us up anymore. When we were little, our mom would dress us in similar (never identical) outfits. I always had everything in pink and Isa in purple, even our bedrooms. If I got a doll with a red dress, Isa would get the exact same one but in a blue dress. All through last year we were really identical. But over the past few months, especially since school started a few weeks ago, we grew to be very different. Now we're not as close as we used to be.

Isabel has changed her style—from preppy-cute to wearing all-black clothes and changing her hairstyle constantly: dyeing it blue, putting it in cornrows, and now her recent rocker chick mullet. Meanwhile, my hair is still long and brown and wavy, and I wear bright and flowing clothes, kind of hippy-ish. You'd have to look pretty carefully to see that we're twins, even though we're technically identical.

Isabel placed the box carefully on her desk, turned on her gooseneck lamp, and peeked inside the flaps of the box's lid.

"What is it?" I repeated.

Isabel turned and looked at me, considering me for a minute. Then with a little smile on her face she said, "Come see."

I crossed the room, swiveling my head from side to side to look at all the redecorating she'd done in the past few weeks. Unlike my room and the rest of the house, Isa's room was neat as a pin. But she'd covered her purple walls completely with rock band posters and things cut out of magazines: race cars, futuristic skyscrapers, weird artwork, and more. My eyes were like pinwheels during the quick journey to her desk.

I peered over her shoulder, not knowing what to expect. When I spied the box's contents, I gasped and reared back.

"Whoa!" I said. "That's a snake!"

Isabel smiled wider and reached her hands into the box.

"Careful! It might bite you!" I said, clutching my hand to my chest. Despite being the child of two veterinarians, I am not a snake person.

But apparently, Isabel now was.

"It's a corn snake. Corn snakes don't bite," she said confidently.

She pulled her hands out of the box, and in them sat an orange striped snake, coiled neatly into a pile of snakiness. I couldn't believe my eyes.

"OMG. What is that disgusting thing doing here?" I said, jumping backward about four feet.

Isabel's smile faded into its new usual scowl, and she turned her back on me, cradling the snake. "It lives here now," she said quietly, but with a hint of pride in her voice. "With me. I adopted it."

I realized I'd just made a major blunder when I'd called the snake disgusting. I knew I had to apologize, or this would escalate into a huge fight, like all our disagreements lately, and I needed Isa's help to find the comic book. She is the only good finder in the family, and the odds were high that the book was in here, anyway. While her back was turned to me, I scanned every surface, but I didn't see it—not that that meant anything. If Isa had the comic, it would be neatly alphabetized and filed away on her bookcase.

I sighed. "I'm sorry, Isa. It just scared me. I'm . . . I'm just not really a snake person."

"Well, I am. Just because we're identical doesn't mean we're *identical*!"

I put my hands up in surrender. "Jeez, sorry. I never thought we were."

"Look, just don't tell Mom and Dad, okay? I really want it, and, well, you know how they are about pets. . . ."

Our parents laid down the law about pets a long time ago. They are willing to foster animals briefly, and we have done so many times over the years. (Our most recent foster was a tiny, adorable Shih Tzu called

Gizmo, who my friend Amber wound up adopting.) But despite the many, many times that Isa and I begged to keep the fostered animals, our parents always maintained that we did not need any permanent pets at home. They said it'd be too much work for them to take care of animals all day at their clinic and then come home and do it again at night. In a moment of weakness my mom once admitted that she'd made the rule early on because our dad was such a softie that our house would have looked like Noah's ark if she'd let him start keeping animals.

"Do you really think you can have a secret pet? That seems like a bad idea," I said.

Isabel's eyes were huge and earnest. "Please, Sisi? Please let it be our secret?"

She hadn't called me Sisi in ages. I melted. "I guess. I just think it's a bad idea, but I won't say anything. At least, not for now."

Isabel released a breath she must've been holding for a while. "Thank you."

Just then the doorbell rang downstairs. Isabel looked at me, alarmed, but then her face changed as she seemed to realize who it was.

"Could you please go get the door for me? It's

Francie—the girl I'm adopting the snake from. She has the tank and all the gear and stuff. I need to stay up here with the snake, just in case Mom and Dad randomly come home. I don't want them to see Naga."

I raised my eyebrows, which are thick and dark and make quite a statement when I use them like this.

"Please, Sierra? Answer the door?" Isabel begged, her own dark eyebrows knit together on her forehead.

This was practically the longest conversation we'd had in weeks, and I liked having Isabel need my help. Plus, if she felt like she owed me one, she'd probably help me look for my comic book.

"Okay," I said, and I dashed downstairs.

I opened the door to find a redheaded girl I recognized from the grade above me at school.

"Hi," I said.

The girl looked at me in confusion. I don't look like exactly Isabel (at least, not anymore), but enough that people do a double-take the first time they see me.

I smiled. "I'm Sierra, Isabel's twin. She sent me down because she's busy with the . . . ah . . . *snake* . . . upstairs." I whispered the word "snake" as if my parents had listening devices everywhere.

"Hi, I'm Francie. This is the gear for Naga." In her arms were a big fish tank with a lamp and some other electrical equipment, plus a little bowl and a small cavelike shelter, and more.

"Ooh!" I said, spying a white cardboard Chinese take-out container in the tank. "Does Naga eat Chinese food?"

Francie looked perplexed and then she laughed. "No! Those are frozen baby mice. *That's* what she likes to eat! Mice cream! Micecicles!"

Oh no. I actually almost gagged. "O-kaaaay...."

Francie looked at me seriously. "Corn snakes are constrictors—they like to wrap around their prey and strangle it, then eat it. Pretty soon, Naga will have to be fed small live animals...."

I felt weak. I think my jaw must've dropped open because Francie was suddenly eager to leave.

She thrust the gear into my arms. "Thanks so much for taking her. My parents just did not want a snake in the house, but they were really happy to hear she was coming to live with two vets."

"Right," I said. *But the vets don't know it yet,* I added silently. "Well, thanks. Come back and visit anytime!"

Francie turned and walked down the path, waving as she went. She couldn't get away fast enough—I think she was relieved to be done with the snake. She practically skipped down the sidewalk when she left.

"Hmmm," I said, closing the front door with my foot. "I bet we won't see her again." I held the tank away from me at arm's length. If I caught even one whiff of the "mice cream," I would surely be sick.

Upstairs, Isabel startled when I came in.

"It's just me, relax," I said. I put the gear down on her bed. "Um, do you know what this critter eats?"

Isabel smiled. "Yup."

I shuddered. "Are you going to keep it in the freezer, like, with all of our food?"

She nodded. "Uh-huh."

I sighed. "It's a good thing our parents are so messy. They'll never notice."

"I know. But they might notice the tank. I'm going to work to get this all set up before they come home. It's going in my closet."

"Well, at least they're super-busy right now. That should buy you some extra time this afternoon," I said. Our parents were in the middle of renovating one of their examining rooms and their lab area. Though they usually work seven days a week, things right now were crazier than ever, with the renovations going on after clinic hours, making their days really long.

"Mm-hmm," agreed Isabel.

She put Naga back in the cardboard box, carefully closed it, and weighed down the top with a heavy book. Then she came over to the bed to assess what Francie had brought. I hovered in the doorway, unsure if I should stay or go. Isabel never hangs out with me or my friends anymore and her new friends are all kind of weird: either punk and goth and a little scary-looking or soccer-maniac boys from her all-boys travel team. (At first the coach didn't want Isa on his team. But then she played so well he couldn't say no.) We used to have so many little secrets and rituals—we were "Team P," the Perez sisters. "Sisters for life," we would always say, then we'd do a fist bump and pulse our hands away like jellyfish. But that had all dried up lately. It seemed like Team P was on permanent vacation.

I was enjoying feeling close again for the moment,

so I tried to stretch it out. "Remember when we really wanted to keep that German shepherd puppy?" I said.

Isabel smiled briefly. "Roman. He was so handsome."

"Yeah," I agreed, remembering how much we'd loved snuggling with him on the sofa in front of the TV. "But he did have that peeing problem. . . ."

Isabel laughed, a quick, short laugh, but still a laugh. "And when he peed on Mom and Dad's bed, they finally said they'd found him a new family! Funny timing, right?"

"I wish we had a pet," I said wistfully.

"Well, now we do!" cheered Isabel.

"Humph. A snake's not really a pet. I've always wanted something furry to snuggle with."

"I think a snake's a pet. I'll snuggle with Naga," said Isabel defiantly.

"Right. Sorry," I agreed, thinking, *Whatever, cuckoo!* Things were starting to get a little dicey, so I figured I'd better strike while I still could. "Any chance you'd help me look for a comic book I lost? It's called *Ms. Marvelous*?"

Without even looking up, Isabel jerked her thumb

at her bookcase. "Bottom shelf. Under the letter *M* for Marvelous. Sorry. I saw it in the living room and thought Mom had gotten it for me."

Bingo! I went to her shelf and pulled it right out. While I was there, I noticed lots of books I'd never seen before.

"Hey! When did you get all into graphic novels?" I asked, fanning them out and showing them to Isabel.

Isabel shrugged. "I don't know. My friends are into them."

"Yuck!" I said, fanning the pages and seeing gore and more gore.

Isabel got annoyed then. "You know what? Just . . . can you just leave? I don't need you in here being all Goody Two-shoes and judging my stuff. Okay? We're not the same person anymore. So just skedaddle! Get out!" Isabel grabbed all the books from my hands, extracted my *Ms. Marvelous* comic and slapped it at me until I took it, and then said, "Shoo!"

I raised my hands in the air in surrender. "Sor-*ry*!" I said, leaving the room. "And I'm not a Goody Two-shoes!"

"Ha!" was the reply before the door slammed shut behind me.

And there I found myself standing alone again in the upstairs hall—but at least this time, I had the comic book in my hand.

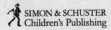

Still Hungry?

There's always room for a Cupcake!

CUPCAKE DIARIES

Emma
all stirred
up!

by coco simon

CUPCAKE DIARIES

Alexis
cool
as a
cupcake

by coco simon

CUPCAKE DIARIES

Katie
and the
cupcake war

by coco simon

CUPCAKE DIARIES

Mia's
boiling point

CUPCAKE DIARIES

Emma,
smile and say
"cupcake!"

by coco simon

CUPCAKE DIARIES

Alexis
gets
frosted

by coco simon

CUPCAKE DIARIES

Katie's
new recipe

CUPCAKE DIARIES

Mia
a matter of taste

CUPCAKE DIARIES

Emma
sugar and
spice and
everything
nice

by coco simon

CUPCAKE DIARIES

Alexis
and the
missing
ingredient

by coco simon

CUPCAKE DIARIES

Katie
sprinkles & surprises

by coco simon

CUPCAKE DIARIES

Mia
fashion
plates
and
cupcakes

sew zoey

Zoey's clothing design blog puts her on the A-list in the fashion world . . . but when it comes to school, will she be teased, or will she be a trendsetter? Find out in the Sew Zoey series: